Jalal Alamgir

Layout Design by Rachel Lambert, rlambertdesign.com

ISBN Paperback: 978-1-970321-10-4

ISBN Hardcover: 978-1-970321-11-1

In loving memory of Jalal Alamgir who was taken suddenly from his family and friends

contents

nose

1994
FEBRUARY 25

SHE HATES HER NOSE. SHE THINKS her nose is a little too big. She thinks the stem is thick, thicker than it should be, and fleshier too. She wants a lank stem, narrow, you know, just the right width, not more than a quarter of the length. She also doesn't like how it bulges out at the tip. The tip's really round, as if she has a small ball stuck inside the skin. And it's soft. It makes her look unfocused and unintelligent. If only she had a nice clear-cut square and thin tip on a narrow stem held at the base of the nostrils ninety degrees from the upper lip, she'd be happy. And her nostrils are too big- not a very feminine thing. Oh, and she hates how her nostrils flare up when she gets excited talking. She's doesn't want to even imagine what other people think of her nostrils. They don't seem to look into her eyes when they speak to her. The bulge and the nostrils, that's what they seem to concentrate on. And they enjoy it; don't they realize that it's impolite to keep on staring at someone's nose when there should be eye-contact? And it disgusts her to think how just a nose, a stupid disfigured cursed nose, can sometimes screw up her whole body language. She decides that from now on she's going to keep a low profile. She will be very controlled and calm and zen-like and talk slowly and never get so excited that her nostrils heave up and down. Maybe if the nose were not naturally placed in the middle of the face, things would be different. Why did we have to have a nose, of all things, as the center of our facial topography? An evolutionary bungle; that's what it is. Well maybe not, she pauses, it's useful to have it near your mouth, so you can smell what you eat, but still, it should not grab people's attention like the way hers does. Oh, why the devil did she have to have such a disfigured nose? Her parents are the ones to blame, it's not that she had a genetic choice about her nose. And now she has to live with it. It's a bad joke, of very poor taste. Sometimes, standing in front of the mirror, she wishes her parents were dead. No, not dead, she takes it back. She wishes they were different people, yes, better looking ones with better looking noses. She probably got that unshapely nose from her father. He has a big fat nose. Now it goes well with his ridiculous belly, but she herself is slim. And yes, that's the main problem: her nose just doesn't go with the rest of her body. Why didn't she get her mother's nose? It wouldn't be perfect, but it sure would be much better. At least it wouldn't be as fat. She likes the width of her mother's nose. She knows she could have lived with it. If she had a million dollars, like from a lottery or something, the first thing she'd do is get a plastic surgeon have her nose fixed.

birth

1995

I'M COMING, I'LL BE THERE

From lot of activity and movement, needed to come out early
Water broke, what is this
Fever, lot of fever
Local MBBS docs panicking, have to send to Khulna, but road crap
Have to send to Dhaka, but can't move
Fever doesn't go down
Police Chief came, saw, vomited
Went to Hai shaheb, he heard it all, referred to Pir Baba
Went to Pir baba, said I'll only come if there is good sign, vanished for 2 days, came put hand on pet
Brought back to hospital in the middle of night, four people took her down the steps
Hospital scene, lot of poor, Sister Fatima, Sister Angela
Finally normal birth

the room

1996
APRIL

PERCHED ABOVE A LITTLE WALKWAY LEADING into the meadows, was a spacious room, a bright, happy room made for Fall afternoons-- its rug crimson, couches orange, windows yellow with maple leaves turning color, and its wooden floor, true Adirondack pine, a gleaming golden.

We had been sitting in the room since dinner. We knew we both had errands to run, but neither wanted to be the first to leave. We were fixed, somehow on a strange wavelength, attracted not to each other but to the pure tension that exists between a lustful boy and a girl. Slaves to the occasion, we sat there, simply sat there, apparently watching tv, but deep down, just being, just living, unable to do anything but be.

"New kids on the block-- they're so young." Anna had more opinions than I.

"Yeah, they are." All my opinions were hers.

"Ozzy Osbourne is so fucking weird."

"Yeah he is. I heard he eats live birds on stage."

To a teenager, this is romance. He doesn't need poetry; a basic ability to converse is enough. He doesn't need low cut dresses; he simply needs to look at a girl with a semblance of breasts. That is the beauty of the teens. I wanted Anna. She had an amazing bosom for such a young girl, pushing through the plain t-shirt she was wearing. She was laughing at the anthems on Mtv, and I watched with her, laughed when she laughed, nodded with her complaints, did everything to show we were compatible, that there was rapport in the room. Sometimes I glanced at her legs, smooth and shaven, exposed wonderfully in small khaki shorts. I found her, once a while, peeking at me from the corner of her eye. The urge inside me swelled, and my stomach ... it felt so deliciously, uncontrollably, empty. I was weightless. I wanted to flutter over and kiss her. In my mind I was already, but my legs, hulks of lead, didn't move; I just couldn't muster the courage.

Is it right? I kept thinking. Is it appropriate? Most importantly, is it legal?

My college orientation fed me heaps of bad advice. In small groups and big crowds, in classrooms, auditoriums, quads, we were lectured, counseled, brainwashed, and warned, delicately, expressly, repeatedly: Do not, do not, do not. *Restrain thyself.* We had to learn the ropes of a civilized society. The foreign students were taken to a correctional facility called Clarkson University, where vanloads of new foreign stock congregated from schools around to be given instructions on how to experience America. It was our version of Ellis Island. Through those tours and talks vanished the delight of discovering a new place in a simple human way. Imagine: Americans on an exotic island, huddled like sheep, led around and addressed for days on the code of conduct.

I found, not surprisingly, that my first month in the Land of the Free had turned me into a meek little lamb.

Etiquette. Maintain the protocol of gender relations, or you are a harrasser. Here is the definition, memorize it: *Copulation is a capitalist contract between an independent erect penis and an independent saturated vagina to form an association until such time that one party deems the merger over, upon which, for further interaction, one must seek a renewal of the entire contract, validated only by an explicit verbal consent of both parties in a sane, sober and somber state.* And so on.

I was truly intimidated by the volume of insipid exchanges that seemed to be involved in courtship, and feared that somewhere along the line I would surely lose my hard-on. I felt like chickenshit even though Anna was not American, Hungarian. And so ensued another pathetic pick-up conversation.

"Ahem ... what are you thinking?" I asked Anna after I couldn't take anymore. I had to say something, and the question seemed harmless enough to start. Prompted by courtesy, she might also ask me what I was thinking, just as people say, "I'm fine, and how are you?" Then I could freely tell her I wanted a fuck. *Not my fault, you asked, I didn't harrass you.*

Sure enough, Anna asked me what I was thinking.

"Er... I was thinking, well, that it would be kind of nice to kiss you."

"Why don't you then?"

I was shocked. Permission? So quickly? No signature, no affidavit of purpose!

I was thrilled as I had been never before. My fingers quivered as I leaned over; my cheap thirdworld shirt could hardly conceal my pounding heart.

We kissed. In the dim crimson of the room, we kissed, and kissed with a passion that comes abundantly with immaturity. For several minutes we explored each other, our tongues intertwined. My neck ached from leaning upon her, but no matter; my hardness kept. I asked her to come to my room, led her along the hallway, and once inside, decided to keep the affair dark. The light remained off. The gentle glow of the moon trickled in, and we, I eighteen, she sixteen, were on fire.

We were free of clothes, free of color, of light, tension, thought, or concern for the future, but most of all, we were free of clothes. Anna's young, nude body was butter, her curves perfect, her silhouette simply divine. I kissed her wildly. I caressed her. I grabbed and groped her, squeezed her and massaged her. I did everything I wanted to do without thinking a blink. She was very docile. I began to wonder if she was enjoying it as much as I was, and then began to doubt. Again, no matter; my hardness kept.

We were perched above a little walkway leading into the meadows, consummating desire, living a bright, happy moment made for decadence--our blood crimson, eyes aflame, and our ecstatic hearts, true youthful hearts, a gleaming golden. That is all I remember.

That Anna died the next morning. Or was it Helen? I don't know, could it be Karinne? I don't know, oh my head, my head, it's hurting again, I don't know, stop, stop, please stop, please don't question me, please stop asking me, I don't remember anymore, I just don't.

I want to go to sleep now.

Can I? Can I go to sleep? I like to sleep.

airport hotel

1997
SEPTEMBER 2
DHAKA

The dinner table at Airport Hotel is where serious social ills are discussed by a menage of doctors, professionals, politicians, politicial scientists, economists, executives, entrepreneurs, students, and even enlightened housewives. Airport Hotel is a den. People flock here at the end of day's work to take drugs, but instead of opium, they dope on opinions. Dinner is served, always with a good dose of opinions, on the second floor, where Nanu, the aging matriarch, reigns. Around dinner time, the staff from the third and fourth floors, including Akhtar, descend gingerly to the dining room to wait on the doped up luminaries. Airport Hotel has a distinct culture: it is an incarnation of the Coffee House of Calcutta, maybe Greenwich Village of New York or, perhaps a turn-of-the-century opium den in Shanghai.

In Airport Hotel, people have to be fed in batches because the table seats only eight, and even that when people are closely packed together. Everyone has a preferred seat. Moni Khalu, of course, gets to eat with the first batch. He would sit to the left of Abba, who would hunch over his food at the head of the table. The other end would be honored by Taufiq Khalu, who would crack jokes sometimes and laugh heartily at other times. But most of his attention would be on his two little boys; he'd continuously feed them what he's eating if they happen to be nearby. Moni Khalu, between morsels, would always complain to Abba that Awami League is not politicizing its rule enough, that we need more like-minded people in crucial positions, that the closest policy ranks are infiltrated by the enemies of the nation, and so on. Abba would listen, either packing food in his mouth in rapid succession or chewing on bones leisurely. He would say little. Dipu Khalu, usually seated next to Moni Khalu, would sometimes agree with him, and other times, sound his own opinions about which minister should be replaced with whom, and which doctor is ruining the reputation of both the medical profession and the political party. I would usually speak if something outlandish has happened, or if I find I strongly disagree with something. Airport Hotel has a distinct culture.

delite cinema hall

1997
SEPTEMBER 7
NEW DELHI

IT IS HOT AND MUGGY, AND we are all sweating profusely in front of the ticket booths.

"No more, no more, sold out," shouts a clerk from the counter, and quickly pulls the shutter down, before the crowd can respond.

We are probably five hundred people crammed in a space meant for fifty. On either side, left and right, there are two sets of iron gates that lead into the theatre. Both are completely shut. The one to our right seems to be the regular entrance, with stronger defense. A potential intruder will have a difficult time. He will have to negotiate two uniformed sentries, looking stern and dutiful. Then somehow he will need to cut through a strong grille secured with steel chains and a padlock, and finally, break open a wooden door locked and barred from inside.

Above the door, a lightbulb painted red begins to blink over a sign that says, "House Full."

The crowd is impatient. Our collective perspiration has filled the room with a nauseating stench. The walls, dull yellow and dirty, are radiating a vintage hue, but reeking of an unpleasant history of overwork and underpay. The room has no arrangement for a queue, everyone is moving about freely, fireflies under the blinking light. Many have converged at the door, and together, become a gentle, slow battering ram, thrusting with great force, but at glacial speed. The two guards are denying passage with great valor, and great effort.

The other door seems shut permanently. I squint to see a wooden sign tacked clumsily onto it: "The Air Conditioning Plant is out of order. It is under repair now. We are sorry for the inconvenience. Sd/- The Management." The sign is old. It looks like a permanent fixture. It has cobwebs.

Around me, everyone is cheery.

"Only fifteen minutes to go!" exclaims a happy, young fellow.

"They should open any minute now," a boy next to him declares. He looks like a college student, a rucksack slung casually from his shoulder. One of his buddies whispers something to a third friend, pointing at a group of girls standing quietly in a corner. One of the girls starts to giggle.

Suddenly, the cheerful hum is broken by screams and shouts.

"What happened?" asks a bearded face next to me, too close for comfort.

"I don't know. Why is he shouting?"

The door has opened partly, but a sentry is standing on the threshold, furiously blocking entry. He is waving his fist and shouting from the top of this voice.

"He's gone berserk!" Someone cries from behind.

The guard jumps out of his post by the door, bursts into the crowd and starts slapping everyone.

"Why are you breaking the queue?" Slap!

He leaps at another poor fellow: "Get back into line, you *chutia*."

Slap! Slap! Right on someone's face.

He turns quickly on his heels. He has the look of a satisfied madman on his face, as if relishing this opportunity to vent his daily frustation. Launching a barrage of obscenities, he starts punching with both hands, on whomever happens to be in harm's way. So big and huddled is the crowd that there is hardly a missed shot.

We panic like prisoners of a concentration camp, trying to run in different directions, raising our hands to save ourselves from the guard on rampage. A moustached thug, dressed presentably in a white polo shirt and khaki trousers, joins him promptly, throwing random punches. As I try to jostle myself toward a safer-looking niche, I see a brand label stitched on his shirt pocket; it says, 'Ruf n Tuf.' Someone, probably a veteran cinema-goer, whispers behind me, "He's the manager; he's the worst."

At the narrow door to the main theatre room, its collapsible iron gates almost closed again, another sentry --apparently a non-violent one--waves hastily to a group of frightened young women clustered together:

"Ladies, Hello. Hello, please. Come this way only. Ladies, any ladies, please?"

He shoves them through the door, but expertly blocks a boy who tries to use the opportunity to get past. The boy gets two slaps, garnished with an acute insult to his mother.

But the ladies seem much relieved to be out of the pandemonium. They are smiling, looking at us from inside.

After all the women get to sanctuary, hand-picked by the sentry inside, the gates are pulled apart, and everyone is let in generously. The crowd had been very docile --surprisingly so-- as if people are used to such chaos. They never hit back. They are cheerful again: the show, 'Pardes', is going to start. In a very disciplined way, stark contrast to the anarchy just two minutes ago, they calmly show their tickets, go through the gates, and through the security scan machine, one after another. The city is supposedly fighting a battle with terrorists suspected to be lurking in our midst, threatening na-tional security. There are metal detectors everywhere. But people are used to militant politics in their lives. They don't bother; the metal detector is just another piece of furniture.

Everyone takes seat, guided by crisscrossing beams of flashlights. I squeeze my way past a dozen legs toward a vacant seat, attractively draped in industrial-strength rexin. It's clean. I sit down timidly, still flustered about the mayhem that ended just as abruptly as it began.

We wait, brimming with anticipation, a huge, dark room filled with slapped people, everything quiet but the steady drone of two dozen turquoise electric fans hanging overhead.

The projector begins to whir, and a hand-written greeting appears, slanted and out of focus, on the giant screen.

"Delite-- Delhi's first cinema hall where we show Hindi movies in real stereophonic sound."

The slide changes crudely, and the next message appears-- this one with better focus, but a worse slant.

"Thank you for choosing Delite and for being our true patron."

The slide changes again and the message repeats in Hindi.

father

1998

My father is the most impersonal character in the world.

Don't get me wrong: he is kind-hearted. He has been helping the genuinely poor with a generosity that is nothing but natural. He could be so much worse. He could be cruel; he is not. He could be a criminal; he is not. He could be stupid; he is not. He could be pious; he is not. He still calls my mother twice a week when she comes to visit us in America. Yes, my mother tells him beforehand to do so, or at least hint at it in her sharp, intelligent ways, but he obeys dutifully-- and that whole ritual has acquired its own rhetoric that only the two of them understand. He is responsible. He doesn't lapse in his official duties. He is smart, diligent, stately in his dispensation of justice at his *darbar*. People respect him. He loves his children. He talks with us caringly and affectionately. He will try to give us anything we want-- if we ask for it. And he will do it most sincerely. He is proud of us. He misses us: sometimes our absence even makes him feel suddenly empty.

But he is still the most impersonal character in the world.

He is torn. He is pulled to the North by a perverted, leery-eyed demon. A holy winch from deep inside heaven yanks him Southwards. He stretches in both directions. One day he will split. He keeps many secrets. They will spill out in the air like confetti and lie in a pile like raked leaves. They are about him only, his other wishes, thoughts, deeds, and little acts of perversion, some of them people know fuzzily, some so little and mischievous that no one knows. He preciously guards the little secrets; those are his and his alone. And then, when he is completely by himself, when everyone is gone, he becomes free, free and relaxed in his thoughts and being. But, not for long: something else begins to lurk in the distant corridors of his mind. Dad gives in, not thinking; but suddenly he realizes where he is, and what he is doing, and he feels guilty, and he tries to resist it, and he tries again, but he can't-- he gives in, free and relaxed. And he can never make us all understand that he doesn't intend to hurt anyone; he just wishes they left him alone. "But no, that doesn't mean don't come back; i mean do occasionally come back, and I love you, but tucked in the cushion of you all, I just wished I was all alone." He would feel it, but won't say it.

As a result, in his political as well as personal life, he has become an interesting animal: sly yet blunt. My mom catches him most of the time. His rivals do so sometimes. He is impersonal as he is driven by an extreme ambition. He wants to be a businessman, a politician, a writer and a lawyer all at the same time. As such, while he helps genuinely when asked, and unless pointed out, he takes decisions with his ambition in his mind. This ambition results in his reluctance sometimes to *plan* to spend time with his family. When his arm is twisted to spend such time he enjoys it, but promptly chooses to suppress such enjoyment after spending the time.

He is most impersonal, but he still is my father and I love him.

anne

1998
JANUARY 6
COLOMBO

Leaning forward on the dinner table, Anne Ranasinghe, age seventy-three, told me, "I am a lady who likes to do disgraceful things."

I moved uncomfortably on my chair, as if still trying to settle myself at the table. I was thinking of reaching for one of those meat cutlets. I decided to stay put and listen on.

"You know, they invited me to deliver a speech at that new synagogue outside Berlin, the one that was dedicated to the holocaust victims?"

I just say "yes," not sure if it was a question or statement she was making.

"And I spilled the beans," she continued, moving her hands, ten old fingers with with ten old nails, painted white to match the pearls on her ears. "Tough things needed to be said, and I said them."

"Of course you have the liberty. You are not a diplomat, you are a poet," I assure her.

"Some people must have thought it was disgraceful, the way I spoke about the German government. I must show you the speech sometime."

"Oh, I would be very interested." I reach for the cutlet.

Anne likes to talk. I see her three times a day, once at breakfast, served between 7:30 and 8, once at lunch, served very sharply at 1, and once at dinner, served at 8. She's at her most talkative at lunchtime.

The two dogs, Mimi and Jeremy, lazily walk about. They don't get any attention from either of us. Anne is quick to highlight the distinction between dogs and humans: "You must be friendly with the dogs, otherwise..." She points her finger at the door.

"I like animals," I say.

[Anne talks of her family, her husband who died, her children and step children who are scattered all over the globe, her friends from New Zealand, the Dutch girls who stayed with her ("One was very beautiful"), the medical student who used to live upstairs, the Sinhala girl who wants to marry an Austrian boy she knows, the brilliant gay lawyer who used to work at the International Court of Justice, and she's throwing one name after another, and I can't remember any. I don't want her to talk about her most recent forty-five years. I want her to talk about her remote past, I want to hear her tale from before she became part of the high society in Sri Lanka. And she hasn't told me yet. "You must keep the reader guessing, as I told the German Ambassador's wife, you know, the one who writes short stories," Anne says at breakfast the next morning. "Will you pass me the bread please?" she beckons. And I keep on guessing.]

[Anne the old fashioned is suspicious of technology. A German documentary filmmaker once made a film about her life-- they went back to Anne's village and interviewed people. But that movie exists only in spool form, and Anne has declined many requests to transform it to more conventional video. She doesn't have a VCR, though on several occasions I have tried to persuade her to buy one.]

a methodological debate

1999
APRIL 4, MAY 11
PROVIDENCE

"I'M BORED."

"You are? What would you like to do?

"Nothing. I need to be entertained."

"What might entertain you?"

"Tell me something new."

"All right. But to do that, I'll need to do two things."

"What?"

"I have to figure out first what would be *new*, something you don't know, and then, tell it."

"Ok."

"I got it! I bet you don't know what John Travolta's first line was as an actor. Do you know it?"

"You're right: I don't know."

"Then that would be something new."

"So what were his first lines?"

"He is in a leather jacket-- long hair, dented chin, shadow of beard, looking serious but casual-- and he moves his head and swings his finger at you, and says, 'Get outta my space, toilet face!'"

"That's really funny."

"See? I told you something you didn't know."

"Yes, you did. Thank you. Really? Was that the first thing he said?"

"I don't know, I think so."

"What do you mean you think so? You just told me that, and you don't know it?"

"You only asked me to tell you something new. You didn't say I had to know it."

"Are you trying to trick me?"

"It's not a trick. I am just telling you something you didn't expect. I'm still honest in what I'm telling you, but maybe you aren't honest in what you're hearing."

"What are you saying? It's not my fault that you leave gaps in logic."

"Is it logic or sequence?"

"Sequence, logic, what difference does it make?"

"Well, they are both about order. What comes first in order determines if you can make sense of what comes next."

"Like what?"

"Like in a conversation. Like when we're talking. This conversation. Any line follows the previous line. The previous line precedes the following line. If you say something, I respond, then you reply, and so on. If our responses get mixed in order, we won't be able to make sense. I do you a favor and I say, ok, done; you say, thanks. I say, no problem. You say, bye.

What if our order got reversed? Then if you say, thanks. I say, ok. You say, bye. I say, no problem. Does that make sense?"

"It all sounds idiotic to me. You know, this is classic."

"Classic?"

"You're trying to cover up."

"Cover up what?"

"I don't think you were being honest; and to hide that, you are blaming logic."

"I was not being dishonest. I played by the rules we both agreed on. That's what honesty is about."

"No. You're violating trust. Honesty is about trust not rules."

"But my trust was based on what you asked me to do. And you're judging me for something that is totally, how shall I put it, exogenous, to what this was all about."

"'Exogenous.' That's typical, the kind of word you would use."

"And what is that supposed to mean?"

"Precision to the point of unintelligibility."

"So now you're saying accuracy is wrong?"

"Not accuracy, dishonesty is wrong. But if you're so accurate that you mask things, then you start becoming dishonest."

"I don't understand. If I'm accurate then I'm truthful, very truthful, because I'm representing with exactitude. How can I be dishonest?"

"Because you can be accurate, but you can still be morally trumped."

"Would you mind being a bit more 'intelligible'?"

"You think you are right because you observe rules, because you are precise. For you following structure is the right thing to do."

"What do you mean, right? We're getting into shaky grounds here. Do you mean right as in correct or right as in just?

"You're right, there are two rights, but *you* make them one and the same."

"They are not one and the same. And excuse me-- it is I who just spelled them out as different things. You are totally wrong."

"Wrong as in incorrect or unjust?"

"Both, dammit!"

"See? You put them together, you made it into one thing. Do you think it's an accident that the same word means two very different things? No, they *came* to mean the same thing, from misuse by people like you who conflate correctness with justice, who think being accurate is being honest-- and that, conveniently enough, serves political interests."

"Are you through?"

"Yes, for now. Would you like to offer a rejoinder?"

"I would, but what's the use? You're going to deconstruct it anyway. What's the point of doing anything if you are so cynical?"

"No, I'm not deconstructing. I'm just showing you that a lot of your faith is blind faith. You're not a bad person because you're precise-- but the fact that you don't question where some of your values come from slowly pushes you in that direction."

"How do you know I'm not a bad person already?"

"We can find out. Let me ask you the most basic ethical question. I trust you will give the *right* answer."

"Ok, ask."

"Do you think ethics are absolute or relative?"

"Absolute. Otherwise they are not ethics, they are just another set of gauges and meters."

"Well if you think ethics are absolute, you are already steadfast on the fundamental ethic. You are already morally "good" at the most basic level. But you need to figure out another thing."

"What?"

"Ask yourself if your ethics are truly, as you might put it, *exogenous* to your interest."

"And what interest is that?"

"The interests of rule-makers and rule-followers. You need to preserve the structure that preserves your standing."

"Look, I think you are misjudging me. I don't go by just any structure that so called 'rulemakers' make. There are some good, widely agreed, rules you know."

"There may well be, but widely agreed doesn't necessarily mean good. A lot of your faith comes from data. That's because you want to be safe by shifting responsibility on others. If you rely on hard evidence, you are safe. Whatever the accusation, you can just point to the 'facts' and say, 'look, as anyone can see, I'm right. The facts, the numbers, say so.'"

"Frankly, I don't think I can say *anything* safely now."

"Safely?"

"Yes. Whatever I say, you will try to peel it off like onion."

"So instead of letting me peel, you'd rather be safe and say nothing? No comment?"

"That's right, 'no comment'. I'll be silent. You know why? Because you cannot deconstruct *that*, the absence of language. Silence is the hard reality you can't peel off."

"Except if silence is an expression, constructed for a specific purpose. I see you won't say anything. Jesus! Your lips are truly sealed! Well, let me tell you anyway why you invented the comment, 'no comment'. Because you have a law, a framework, and it falls within it. You have given yourself a constitutional right to express-- right to freedom of speech, and a constitutional right to not express-- right to silence. But you haven't given yourself any right to imply, liable to be inferred. That would get you into trouble. In your world you are always treading railway tracks, following the lines carefully, this way or that, not stepping in the middle. Accuracy sifts good from bad, lies can be sanitized by calling them explanations, made to fall within acceptable parameters, and conclusions run you over like trains. In my world, reality is not urban railroad, but a lustrous jungle of suggestives. Meanings lurk like chameleons."

[Would you believe it if I tried?]

pr guy, the mean green interview machine

1999

MAY

[ELEVATOR]

"So, before you leave this room, if there's one thing that you to want to leave with me about you, one thing that is special about you that I can remember, what would it be?"

"Well," said Guy, leaning back on the chair a little, uncrossing his legs. He paused for a second, then continued, with a smile. "The thing I want you to remember is that I really enjoy interacting with people. If I can get paid for doing it, I'll be doing something I enjoy."

Doing Better

You should be looking for confident people

"What characteristics should someone have, then, to be good in PR? Do you think you have those characteristics rather than just enjoy?" Paul asked. It seemed an important question. I will need a thorough answer, he thought to himself.

"The first characteristic is that your candidate should be a man."

"Er, what do you mean?" Paul asked, a little confused. "You mean rhetorically, like saying "you the man!"? Paul laughed.

"No. I'm saying you need to hire a man. The male of the species."

"Oh really? That's interesting. We do have laws against discrimination. I'm sure you know that and you also know that it's a law we all are very sensitive about, so are you still suggesting that we should hire a man?"

"That law is about the fairness of the process, it has little to do with what you believe is useful for your purpose. You can hire a man and get away with it..."

"Even then, why should I automatically hire a man?" Paul broke in impatiently.

"Educated men are funny creatures." Guy answered, unperturbed. "They love rules. Imagine two people arguing. The woman is pissed, just plain pissed. The man is stiff. Argument makes men stiff. He likes to remind the woman, speaking rigidly, of the sanctity of rules, He uses phrases like, "I acknowledge that you didn't like what I did but I don't understand, I didn't commit a crime?" He speaks like an educator, formally. He likes to sound refined. Structured. Reasoned. Logical. Rules. "I know I hurt you but according to the rules I am not wrong. I'm not violating anything. How am I supposed to know that I hurt you when I know that what I'm doing is ok by the rules we agreed on?" You're a hypocrite, even if you follow the rules, says the woman. The man is quiet. Rather than argue back at something and risk getting morally trumped again, he would stay quiet. In other words, a good characteristic for your PR person." Guy stopped for a second, but implied, by body language, that he's not done;

he's just taking a breather. Paul complied and stayed silent, without realizing the implication. He waited for Guy to finish.

““No comment.” Men invented that comment. It falls within the law. I have a constitutional right to express --my right to freedom of speech, and I have a constitutional right to not express --my right to silence. But I don't have the right to imply, liable to be inferred. That would get me into trouble. Men are moved by the beauty of this black and white. Women hate it because their natural habitat is in that lustrous spectrum of suggestives where meanings are lurking like chameleons in the rainforest, camouflaged in shades of color, known to be there, but not perceived. Men make better spindoctors because they can readily justify their lies by calling them explanations; they don't find any moral problems with it, and they know how to make their explanations appear to fall within the strict parameters of the law. They make better and as long as they tread those lines of meaning and not step in the middle, that realm of ambiguity, their asses are safe. Safety and stability are important to men. That's the kind of impression you want your PR department to give. Frankly, the PR dept is kept for bad times. For good times the executive takes the credit personally and directly. You don't need someone to speak for you. But you gotta find a guy who can handle the bad times. In times of deepdoo, you'll need a guy who can impress by being calm and precise, if necessary, to the point of unintelligibility. You need to hire someone who can look up straight at you and say, “I understand fully the gravity of the synergy between the the male gender's obsession with order and its value for maintaining a stable and predictable relationship with the public. Any other questions?””

“Er.... yea, Yes.” Paul seemed started. He blinked, as if woken up because a sudden question had broken his chain of attention. “Yes, I do have a few other questions,” Paul sat up straight.

“No,” Guy laughed. “I'm sorry, I meant that not as a question, but as something that person should say to you. It was his ... part of *his* statement.”

"Ah," Paul also laughed, slightly embarrassed. "Well, you've certainly made an interesting point about men. I guess you're right, in some ways at least, but there are women who can be like that too."

"Yes. There are women who can be like that," Guy repeated. "But there aren't women who just are like that."

"You mean naturally?"

"Yes."

"Well," Paul let out a deep breath, and looked down at his notes. "Let's see..." he bid for time.

But at the same time, they are inherently more corrupt. This creates an existential contradiction in men.

diary

1999
MAY 6
PROVIDENCE

Dear Diary,

You are a good friend. You are scattered everywhere in my house. When you were younger, about four years ago, you used to be a book of limericks. But my very first memory of you goes back ten years, to 1989, when you were just a blue appointment book with flimsy pages. You have grown since, become well-rounded, multifarious. You're email printouts. You're floppy disks. You're newsgroup threads. You're magnetic poetry. You are preface and acknowledgments. You are stories, doodles, gibberish.

But those are lost, like skin shed by snakes. I didn't keep track while you slithered on to become this, a letter.

Yesterday there was a coincidence. Nagesh was telling me stories about his life. He was supposed to tell me a founding story of his life, something that has made him, a heroic tale of courage, endurance, and survival. Right before he began to speak, he paused. Suddenly he realized it was a myth. Somehow he had constructed, out of pride, accomplishment and a bit of sheer historic negligence, a fable of greater gallantry than what actually happened. The story of "How I Got to Simla," it turned out, took place when he was in the eighth grade, not the sixth. He was puzzled, then crushed, and abruptly, alarmed. I consoled him. "It's ok," I said, "we all have our myths. It's a good myth. And it doesn't make a difference if it happened two years ago or two years after-- it's still a great story." He agreed and was happy again. Later I thought about it and became convinced that it's really fine. Why shouldn't we have myths around us? Should it be just what happened that defines us? Are we facts only, our public life nothing but a curriculum vitae? What about imaginations? Why can't we use them to shape us as well? Why am I concerned that I'm trying to build a bridge between the person I am and the person I want to be? [Ladies and Gentlemen of the Jury, this is an extended remix of my life.]

Nagesh teases me that I have not written any story about him. If he asks me again I will reply, "why, this --this is the record of my thoughtlessness." I am scattered like you, Diary, you will understand. Mirror won't. To him, I am a whole, wholesome person, flesh and blood. But you don't know me that way at all. You know my stories, I have inscribed them on you. Mine are also fact-driven. My characters are facets of people I know. My fiction is merely autobiography. I am aware that I can be very creative, as long as I'm writing a book review. Maybe that's my structural limit. That's why in the end I will be monotonous to read, a circular motion in the same arrangement. Thank God I'm scattered. Are others?

I know you can't answer that, Diary. I know you well: answering is not your forte. You're at your best when you describe things for me. You make good conversation until I ask you something. Most people, I imagine, are not honest in everything they do. They also have facades they put on for different occasions. Some are more honest when they speak; those rarely make politicians. Some are honest when they eat. Those become fat. Some honestly mow their lawn, or curse some harami shitbag. And then there are some people who work out with a sincerity I don't get even when I'm taking an exam. They put on a pedometer, heart-rate monitor, skin-tight aerodynamic honeycomb beeswax spandex, mango-color rainbow sneakers with reflector lights, and little rings of lead around their finger just to raise resistance. With a patch of velcro they strap on a yellow waterproof walkman, elastic cordless headphones. Then with jinkychink music, they run, fast. They exercise their hearts out. When they are done, they sweat clean mountain fresh water. Beads of clear vitamins glaze down their chiseled, polished bodies. They have no smell, those honest workers. The breeze from their deodorized armpits remind you of lush meadows in spring bloom, and you spin round in innocence. But I am at my most honest right now. This moment with you, Diary.

Thank you for a good time. It's been real.

Your friend,
Jallu.

missing story name

2000
JANUARY

THE MACHINE CAME, THE DOORBELL RANG; it was time to go.

Niko looked over his shoulder: the bed he was leaving untidy, the lamp on, books scattered on the rug, a bunch of pinball game tokens on the dresser, dresser and its shattered mirror, underwear, socks, newspaper, music, pills, a glove… where's the other? Not on the dresser--in the closet? Oh well. Careful, don't step on the broken glass. Hey there it is. I better take them, I'll definitely need them.

He closed the door, opened it back, turned off the lamp, then locked up and left.

Outside the rain had just stopped. The night was glistening everywhere. Niko liked rainy nights. Somehow the city seems so alive after rain. Thank rain; it kills the mad rush and breathes fresh life. These steps are so slippery! Did I forget my passport? Damn, I should've made a list. Anyway, I have to trust myself. I have it, I know I must've packed it. I can't lose any more time.

Niko ran through Prince Street, fast but not fast enough to stand out. Splish-splash on puddles, zigzag neons, things passing by, so cellulose. The drizzle came back. Wait for walk sign now, there are too many cars. Damn, can I get there by eight? Holy shit! You bastard, you nearly killed me! Fuck! These trucks never stop for pedestrians. Asshole! Niko cleaned his glasses and looked at his watch one more time, just to make sure that no time has passed for the last five minutes. He ran.

I have to stay calm when I meet Shikha. I know she'll panic, but I have to tell her straight. I wonder how long we'll have to spend there. I mean I have to convince her, and then we need to be out, rapido. A payphone! No, I can't explain over the phone. Well, she doesn't need to bring much stuff, just three four days of clothes and money. We should be fine after that.

Niko ran, headed for the bridge. In his six years of living in the city he has never crossed the bridge on foot. It seemed much bigger, towering above everything that he was. His school to the left, his favorite coffee shop behind him, he felt orphaned, and very poor. But he was determined. He took out a dollar from his wallet for a soda from Tim's shop. I hope Tim is not there. I don't have the time.

"Shit!" Niko almost lost his balance. Tim was a tall, burly man, with strong arms for a fifty-year old chain smoker.

"What's up? You look crazy, man!"

"Tim, I'm in a rush, ok? I don't have time right now. Sorry."

Tim still held on to his shoulders. Man, come on, let me go. "Is there anything wrong?"

"No, I'm late for my mock thesis defense. I gotta go." Niko pushed him, and before Tim could say anything, ran. "And I have to pick up a soda from your store on the way."

"Jeez, good luck. About time you finished that thesis."

Soda took a whole two minutes, but Niko knew after he crossed the bridge that time doesn't matter any more. If we play it right, time is on our side.

Shikha's neighborhood is not very nice, so he decided to walk. The river smoothly separated the comfortable from the desperate. Looking around nervously … I hope I don't get mugged. This bag.

the december evening experiments

2000
DECEMBER 11

The kitchen was dimly lit by holiday lights: six or seven little plastic cars, lightbulbs inside, strung around some shelves with green bottles of Rolling Rock beer. Three bottles. Tall, medium and small. "Papa beer mama beer and beer cub," he smiled. He pulled the chair and sat down, rather precariously, since the metal chair was in a bad, rickety, shape. And it won't be a good impression to fall off a chair around people you are just getting to know. You don't want to convey any sense of imbalance. So, carefully, he crossed his legs. He lit a cigarette, let out a puff of smoke, gently, as if he's now in control of his surroundings. He looked around, slowly moving his head, panning his eyes, absorbing the view, small talking. Then he saw the cat. It was a good sign, he thought. It is good to have something to toy with, magazines, or even a cat, when silence sometimes gets awkward around semi strangers. The striped animal was nonchalant, as cats can be to strangers - the complete opposite of canine personality. It leapt up on the counter, and almost didn't make it. It too had a problem with balance; it was pregnant. The kittens inside its big belly must have felt a strange elevating sensation. The cat climbed, this time gracefully, to the windowsill. And that was the perch. It had started to snow outside. Half an hour later, half an hour's worth of short foggy moments later, he looked up again, eyes red. "There is no way an animal can look out the window for so long and not think anything," he muttered.

The world was moving a little too fast, like you see from a speeding car the same scenery shoot by again and again, but only a little too fast. Where is he going? Are people speaking English? Wasn't he just asked something? He couldn't understand it, there was a lot of lip movement, he clearly saw. But there seemed to be just vowels and high-pitch sound and some disturbing noises in the back; he couldn't make out what though. And then he realized that both the girls were singing at twice the normal speed.

It's late. He thought it would be nice to walk in the rain now. Maybe he could go to the jogging park on that boulevard street, what's-the-name, ah Blackstone, that's it, Blackstone Boulevard. Sounds respectable. It has big trees. But the park will be muddy. Well, certainly along the trails, so he has to walk on the grass. That shouldn't be too bad. But then it's a ten-minute walk to that park itself. Should he drive that distance? No, that's silly. Maybe he should take an umbrella just in case the rain gets too heavy. But wait, he can't go. She's supposed to call. He doesn't want to miss her call, as she doesn't call much. He will stay.

It hasn't snowed since the first day of the December evening experiments. Now it's January, a year has passed in a couple of weeks, and some things are not the same. He has seen both of them naked. Strange still, but not a stranger. He has played with them, run his fingers through their pubic hair. But he hasn't really known them, either of them. The one you want you can't have and the one you have is not the one you really want. Now it's January halfway through. It's snowing today. But he will not go by his favorite purple house. Two roads diverged in a wood and I took the one less travelled by, just to see if it makes a difference. Frost inside, and Frost outside, too.

hedonism in a catacomb

2002

One day I was depressed, and these are the thoughts I had:

Companies and star trek—they are both right. We should just give up, give all up to companies for now and wait for the replicator to rescue us a few hundred years later. The other day I was sitting, which is an activity that I've become accustomed to doing most evenings. And meanwhile I usually leave all lights, all fans on, all windows open, so there is still plenty of activity around me. I keep channels of communication open too: my email program checks for new messages at five minute intervals, a messenger software tells me when my friends come online and when they leave, the browser page refreshes every few minutes, the computer speakers continuously blare out obscure compositions from online radio. With my CPU whirring and hard drive downloading long media files in the background, I sit, news-ed out, and banner-ed out.

(I chose my news ticker from a Yahoo advertisement banner.)

And then I get tired, suddenly.

I was doing all this and more the other day and I needed to take a break. So I walked into the living room, where the TV was on. And I sat again and stared at the screen for a while until on the TV Guide channel a booming voice announced, "With so many channels to choose from there's only one choice you can make: TV Guide."

How right! They are exactly right. How can they not be right? They in the end earn all the money, they ultimately spend the money, they own politicians, goons, they buy most of the most analytical brains in the country, and then they buy their secrecy. These hired brains do research for them, marketing, product development—everything. So they have to be right on the mark. They know exactly how my mind works. They know how helpless I am in this over-stimulated competition-crazy economy. And increased candor all around being one of the major bequests of the last two decades, they are proud to admit it. They flout wise restrictions, they enjoy any lifestyle, any morality they want; they don't even have to hide themselves. I sit there and watch the ridiculous vulgarity that there are so many channels to choose from that there is only one choice to make: watch it all at once. Be swept off, and engulfed in this massive orgy of sound, pictures, and alphanumeric digits, just so you know what is happening where. You are a vessel. The default purpose of your unenlightened life has become to absorb data, keep abreast of things. You have let the explosion of information debilitate you, and completely take you over by persuading your senses to accept arbitrariness as your supreme moral guide and indecision as your capable practical tool to manage life.

Mark my word: this collective hedonism is not bad. Why should it be? What are the criteria for good or bad? Who decides? Nobody can make such a monumental decision. Even if you say it is not right to be arbitrary, it is still correct to be arbitrary. It is politically correct, philosophically logical, and psychologically a very effective emotion dampener. Who would have known that flexibility would become an opiate more powerful than religion?

There is nothing we can do. We will never know what to do, what the right option would be, the one choice to make. Certainly we can't do it alone, we need numbers, for we need to match their power. But as soon as we think we have an inkling of what needs to be done, we will get overwhelmed by the burden of information we need to muster and distribute to persuade everyone to do it with us. It's too late for social remedies. We just have to sit and watch. One day technology will lift us off into a more pleasant future.

Enter the "replicator" from Star Trek. It is the ultimate device for it can replicate whatever one wants. It gives choice back to the user of the device. Note, the use of the word "user" and not the "consumer". As it focuses on providing utility which is a derivative of choice. It is the opposite of consumption.

The best dupe is the hopeless liberal. Sigh.

Then I went to sleep. The next morning I woke up, cheery from knowing that I know.

new job.

2004
FEBRUARY 13

When I joined—it was a Tuesday, not a traditional Monday—I was nervous. And shy: I stayed indoors, sitting in my office, with the door just slightly ajar to show that I am in and working. I didn't sleep the night before the first day of classes, even though I considered myself prepared. I was torn. My office was all governmental off-white and steel, the shelves, desks, chairs, and the file cabinet, all colored to match. The spray-painted enamel on the furniture, camouflaged against the flat coat of the wall, formed a seamless industrial landscape: awash in overhead fluorescent light, jagged rectangular shapes protruded rudely out of still air. The plaster and metal stunned me, but I found it strangely reminiscent. I would get that feeling on windy January mornings, staring at the I-93 flyovers from below, those massive, green, metallic structures, carrying hundreds of cars, producing a constant, loud whisper of tires against asphalt.

I settled into my office, on my small green task chair. As a graduate student, I had one exactly like it, in black. As a graduate student I would have been grateful. As a business consultant I was disappointed. I approached everything with a quiet attention, showing my studious, absorbing side while hiding a nagging disapproval. Yet, in my calm, I must have come across as cheaply corporate.

I overcompensated in conveying self-assurance, so that I am not taken as lightly as I look young. I took it out on them.

inter*na*tional rela*tions*

2006

Anarchy

As a starting point, anarchy is a useful concept. It is apparent that no higher authority exists over the state. Even though authority is created (mostly by the dominant states), states frequently flount them. The state is God. And by extension, the cabinet is God.

Paradox

If states frequently flount authority, but they also want to point to higher authority when they are questioned by those they are held accountable to. That means the state functions to serve the needs of the elite for them to stay in power.

Democracy

There is no democracy. It is always governed by an elite. Democracy is only process. It is a means to regularize the struggle for power (and thereby minimize risk) among different members of the elite. That is its essence; everything else is a detail.

Order

War and peace are the opposites of the same coin called order. A binary variable, members of a mutually exclusive set-- they are both. We are explaining war and peace only because we are interested in order. That is the track that the discipline has followed.

Theory

A discipline does not necessarily have to have telos. But that does not mean we cannot analyze what has happened. The absence of telos makes future indefinite, but that does not mean we cannot stand at the present and look back at the past to describe, discuss, explain, and critique, that is theorize. Explanatory theories are positivist. Critical theories generate a different kind of knowledge. So do discursive theories, mainly known as narratives.

Narrative

Narrative is the path of knowledge. International Relations (IR) has a narrative which documents and charts the path it has taken in the project of generating knowledge. While it has tried to explain 'reality', it has also created it in our minds. It is not without reason that the narrative has used the images and icons that it uses to describe and explain the world-- images like polarity, order, anarchy, system, unit, structure, agent, dependence, interdependence, regime, absolute gains, relative gains, sovereignty.

Ontology

In the end, IR is about seeing the world only through a particular lens, at a particular level of social interactions and an even narrower level of existence. It cannot progress beyond a certain point without altering some of the most basic assumptions, values, and starting points. Both the reality and the narrative have limited the potential of its development. It cannot evolve into intergalactic relations because it holds humanistic behavioral assumptions.

Epistemology

Social theories are a must in intelligent species able to reflect and learn. We cannot get rid of them. Despite their awkwardness and their fancy leaps of faith, we need them. Understanding is comfort. But it will still be many more years till we can have a grand theory able to generate understanding at levels so deep that we will become just brains: we would be reflective, learning brains working at paces unimaginable, staying alive, pulsating, just to think; every other task is delegated to machines, artificial intelligence of our own creation. A grand theory would mean two things. It would mean that we can finally have a clear sense of everything. Anything of which we can have a clear sense, we can teach - for teaching and making sense of the world are the same thing. And anything we can teach in a clear sense, we can teach machines to do, for we can express it in mathematical terms. Knowledge of the grand theory would make humans and machines equal. At the same time the grand theory will explain their evolution into becoming equal. The theory would have to explain itself. It cannot stand outside it. That is why it cannot be positivist.

trial

2007

I DON'T HAVE A FIRST LINE, Your Honor, but I can tell you that I am into definitions nowadays. Let me draw an analogy: literature is lush, lavish use of words. Even when minimalist, it succeeds by taking an opulent journey into the realm of ideas. What matters the most is not the ideas, but the opulence, the "wordly" existence. Simply, that is the promise of a literary work. Your Honor, you must agree that an important rationale for literature is the reader. It is meaningless if it loses the reader, if it cannot take the reader into extravagance. Really, I have hurt no one, for I have no reader. My works were meant for me. There was no witness. I, the accused, am your only lead.

This is an exam, is it not? I am standing in front of you, you are assessing my statements, ready to use anything I say against me. No scope for faux pas here-- every dot of the i and every cross of the t is ominous, unfriendly. Yes, I remember exams. Here comes the question! Pen in hand, feet down firmly on the floor, sat up straight, I am ready. Alertly I think, quickly I write. I go on, flip the page, and write some more. The margins are generous on all sides. And here is the answer to Question No. 2, written in one paragraph, crisp:

The biggest burden of guilt a true scholar carries is the feeling that he is stating the obvious. He needs to tell himself that he is not. He needs to remind himself of the utility of years of hard work, especially because all took place in dreams, all are imaginations. Yesterday Mr. Prosecutor showed you Exhibit A. He said it was a deadly weapon, a sharp instrument, and he said there are more from where it came. But my arsenal is nothing but concepts and notions, axioms, analogies, *definitions*, proposals and conjectures. Obvious is a statement like this: Scholarship is lush, lavish use of ideas. But what matters the most to you, to the reader, is the destination. My musings are meaningless if they lose destination, if they cannot propel you to *jump* to conclusions.

I admit, Your Honor, that I held the weapon in my hand, and had there been a reader, I might have told him to jump, but only because there is no other way. We have to jump. Logic is neither smooth nor fluid. We need to hop our way from assumption to conclusion. We skip from comma to comma, frisk from chapter to chapter, website to website. Those who try to resist are sued, and you bring them promptly to justice. But my friends, if one does not have a reader, one can easily forget telos. You need not resort to logic to make sense to yourself. Often you do it instinctively, intuitively, without the hopscotch. When you are all alone, you can shed logic like you shed clothes. In private, logic does not make things right or wrong; it is an ethical choice.

Take my case, for instance. In recent years, I have learned to dwell in the realm to ideas. Not action, no, I hardly acted-- but I became acutely aware of what was ethically right and wrong. I was earning a degree, at a good school. I spent my days sitting, thinking, writing, imagining, sometimes reading. To keep from getting fat, I tried to exercise. Every other day I played tennis. I would ride my bike to work, do some thinking and writing there, and after checking email sufficient times everyday, I would ride my bike back home. Each week I ate a few meals outside, trying to inject a variety of junk: pizza, taco, hamburger, falafel, chinese, indian, greek, cambodian. I cooked other meals myself; chicken legs and rice was a recurring theme on my stove. I topped the day with a vitamin pill. I read literature, wrote scholarship. I went to bed, affecting no one, being affected by none. Why bother?

I expected it all to change, and it did not. I expected to graduate from a meaningless existence to a more meaningful one. I did not act toward it. I expected that someone will attend to all that, evaluate me, offer me a job, a good life, and in essence I will have worked for nothing-- promotions, relationships, all taken care of. The unfeasibility of my lofty ideals was disturbing me. I was troubled, going through a depression I hardly admitted. If it is misfortune or my own making I am not quite certain yet. But for you, ladies and gentlemen, the evidence is clear. Of course, who else but I could have done it?

I have a feeling of futility. Whatever I tell you will be in vain. In your world we who question sanity make either criminals or madmen. The conclusion is foregone. This stage, this drama is meaningful to you only, not me. The footlights are there to give you clarity and direction, to disinfect your conscience, but they blind me. Make no mistake. You will be wasting your time if you think you can convince me. We are the victims of your sobriety, and we are certainly aware of our lapse. We know the implications. We know the moral quandaries, the irrationality. But what is sane anyway? Where is the boundary? Is there one?

I am aware, but not in a way you want me to be. I know what I have done but not what I am doing. I am a scholar. I live in the past. "Was" was my friend, "Is" is yours. You make the present and fear the future; I cannot stop you. Your Honor, please take the burden off me if you can.

daughters

2011

YOU WILL RARELY MEET A MAN as polite as Altaf, the orderly-cum-handyman at Airport Hotel. He will listen to you obediently and not interrupt you. As you voice your wishes, sitting back on that easy-chair, he will softly say yes sir or *ji bhaiya*, depending on how old you are.

"Altaf, get me a cold drink."

"Yes sir."

"Get us a rickshaw."

"Yes sir."

"*Ei* Altaf, run *jhotpot* to the *chhupri* shop around the corner and get me a cigarette—Marlboro, the real one, not a fake, ok? Don't buy it if the logo is off-color, and careful, do not hand it to me if my auntie is around."

"Ji bhaiya."

Altaf gets things done. Moreover, the management has recently found out that when no one is noticing, he can make very good *samosas*, spicy-and-all.

Come in, come in. Airport Hotel welcomes you, you and that pregnant auntie and your fourteen generations of extended family. Sorry, bhaiya, I don't mean to be rude, not even in my thoughts. It's a warm place, our hotel, you'll see. Please, let me take those bags and potlas *you brought from your trip. (Oh! They smell nice!) I will get you tea after I show you your room. Lipton or Ispahani?*

Barely five miles from the international airport, and fully air-conditioned, Airport Hotel functions like a small terminal. Mustached *darwans* stand sentinel at its gate. They keep curious street children from soiling the guests and the goodies that taxis ejaculate throughout the day. Baggage-handlers show up promptly to carry impossible loads on their heads while leaping up the stairs at alarming speed. As the guests make their way through the modest lobby and the cramped passages while vociferously insisting the safe transit of their belongings, they receive welcoming *salaams* and a confusion of scents: disheveled caterers smile, smelling of fish; shy maids exude the sham citrus fragrance of powerful cleansers; attentive servers betray a wisp of cumin as they stand aside respectfully; officials wave passport/ticket and travel tax receipts with a musty bureaucratic odor that can only be spawned by newsprint stored in old file cabinets.

Among the staff entrusted with serving the guests, Altaf is the most important, a favorite of the management for his courteous diligence. Has he ever asked for a raise? I don't think so. Even at Eid, he will smilingly accept any amount that is doled out as holiday bonus. Every morning he dons his favorite red-stripe shirt and helps to prepare the breakfast. He washes the guests' clothes by hand under a rickety faucet, working up whatever lather is on offer from an exhausted green bar of soap. He sets them to dry on the roof, one by one on the clothesline, not satisfied till the assorted colors start flapping about like a festive stream of flags atop the building. He proceeds to accomplish random errands, emptying morning tea trays, or answering the phone with the most gentle "Hello, *as-salaam-ualaikum*" you have ever heard, or fetching rickshaws for guests who would saunter out of the Hotel to pursue their businesses of the day, their plump faces content and bulging bellies filled with *bhaji-paratha* and *rasmalai.*

Toward noon, the wind begins to get so hot that even the summer sweat on Altaf's brow dries off instantly. The house stands empty among betel nut trees and the dejected cawing of an occasional crow. The street hawkers retire in the shade, taking a break from trying all morning to peddle their wares. The heat does not faze Altaf. With a bucket of water and some old torn rags, he gets on his hands and knees and mops the entire house. By early afternoon half the guests return to eat. The management springs to life, goes into top gear, the kitchen the engine room, hustle-bustle and smashes of pots and swishes of knives and clings and clangs of dishes and spoons, spills of water and splats of curry, and shouts after shouts:

"Where's the fish?"

"*Paani*!"

"Quick, or I'll be late."

"Has the driver eaten?"

In that hullabaloo Altaf is everywhere, serving, wiping, cleaning, waiting, pouring, dashing, tripping, cursing (softly) and then, "phew!" Three o' clock. The world inescapably droops to siesta under the scorching afternoon sun. Altaf has a chance to sit down, on a small stool in the kitchen. He drinks a tall glass of water. He eats lunch, leisurely, relishing his *dal-bhat* as usual: a crater full of soupy lentil in the middle of a mountain of rice, piled on a tin plate and sprinkled with coarse salt, and a single fire-roasted red pepper on the side. He stretches. He is tired.

Allah, I wish I could sleep, just for half an hour. But someone will ask for me, I know. Or something will happen and I'll have to run and attend to it. They never take a break, these sirs and their begums and their brats, even in their naps. All right, I have to be patient. There's not too long left. One more day, no, just a few more hours. Just a few more hours.

Altaf reaches for an old black notebook he keeps in a kitchen drawer, but before he is able to pull it out—

"*Ei*, Altaf bhai!" Little Shawkat, another all-purpose worker at the hotel, walks into the kitchen. "Nani wants to see you."

Altaf looks up at Little Shawkat, a twenty-five year old man barely five feet tall, which, along with a baby face that lights up with excitement whenever he speaks, makes him look thirteen or fourteen at best. There is no "big" Shawkat at the hotel from whom "little" Shawkat must be distinguished. His name is attached purposely to that diminutive prefix, just as the sightless beggar around the corner is called Blind Hossain, as though his position in society must be commemorated repeatedly by evoking the permanence of his handicap. "Nani is calling you," urges Little Shawkat. "She's on the roof."

"Okay," says Altaf. *Just a few more hours*. He gets up with an obvious lethargy, and ascends his reluctant body up the stairs. A distant relative of the owner, Nani lives in a room on the top floor of the five-storey hotel—the birdcage, she calls it—and has never left the building for as long as anyone can recall. Occasionally she would take a slow and shaky walk on the roof, supporting her fragile septuagenarian frame on a cane, with an attendant alongside. Some afternoons she would sit on a wicker chair and sip her tea while the staff visit, a *darwan*, a driver or a maid, or Little Shawkat or Altaf. They would tell her their stories, their complaints; they would seek her advice or her prayers, and if things have gone really sour with the management, her intervention. It's her afternoon royal court, and she the benevolent matriarch. They call her Nani: grandmother.

Altaf finds her on her rooftop stroll, struggling yet determined to walk, stopping now and then to catch her breath and look at the flower plants swaying in rows of clay pots. She motions for him to walk next to her. He walks up, but stays two steps behind, out of an innate respect.

"You're leaving tomorrow morning?" Nani asks.

"Yes," says Altaf while nodding.

"For how long will you be away?"

"Just three or four days, I think."

"When is your wife due?"

"Any day. My brother sent a message. It can be even tonight."

"I see." Nani stops to take a deep breath while Altaf watches her with a tinge of concern that he always feels when he sees her walk. She continues: "Who knows, by the time you are back, that Farida Auntie may also have a newborn. She should be in a hospital, not a hotel. Having such a pregnant woman around makes the other guests uncomfortable. And a crying infant will be the last thing we need." Nani shakes her head lightly. "One would think she'd have relatives to stay with in Dhaka City, I mean everyone in Bangladesh has relatives in Dhaka. Instead she's here with her nephew, making life difficult for us. Well, what can we do, she has paid extra and in advance. After all, we're running a business."

Altaf does not say anything. Nani stops, inhales slowly, then looks straight at him.

"Are you nervous?" she asks.

"Yes, a little," he replies, after pausing for a moment.

"It will go well, *Inshallah*. Don't worry."

Altaf stays silent.

"Will there be a doctor handy?"

"Yes, Nani," he says with his head bowed down. *The nearest doctor is an hour away, by boat. He won't come, and anyway, where will I get the money to pay for a house call?*

"All right, listen carefully. I don't want you to get stuck there. We have too many guests now." She produces an envelope and continues, "I have some money here for you. Think of it as a bonus; after all, this is a special occasion. But,"—she lowers her voice—"Make sure you get medical attention, you know, considering what happened the last time."

Grudgingly, Altaf takes the envelope. "I don't need money," he protests after a few seconds.

"It's all right. Use it to take care of things."

He bows. They walk in silence for some time. Somewhere in the hotel a kettle begins to whistle, followed gradually by the sound of ruffled clothes and a gentle tinkle of teacups. "Nani, may I go now? I think it's time to serve the afternoon snacks."

Nani nods, and Altaf heads back to the kitchen. He gets absorbed into another daily flow, working automatically, mindlessly, to orchestrate a collation of tea, rusk, and sweets for the Hotel's guests, who all seem to possess an odd ability to devour anything dished up. At dusk, a melodious *azaan* streams out of distant mosques, tenderly calming down the buzz of daily life. In a single elegant stroke, women cover their head with the flowing ends of their *sari* or *orna.* Busy men suddenly seem reflective. Boys return from playing outside. Street lights are turned on, casting only a feeble glow into rapidly encroaching darkness. The aroma of dinner on the stove begins to waft through the corridors of Airport Hotel.

Unlike afternoon snacks, which are taken in guestrooms, dinner is served in the communal dining area, the same location for lunch absent the frenzy. The table seats eight, but as there are at least twice that many who are in need of a meal, guests have to keep coming downstairs to check for openings. As one leaves another joins: the resulting congregation features new and old faces alike, unsure overnight visitors seated next to more experienced lodgers like Farida Auntie. Over the initially muted evening atmosphere eventually arises a palpable tension, between a typically Bengali hesitation to engage strangers in conversation and an equally compelling urge to discuss politics. Most nights end with a clumsy socialization of sorts, touching on the latest textbook crisis, or perhaps corruption in the electric company, or the secret training of religious militants in which some government high-ups must have been complicit. Disagreements abound, but are never vocalized forcefully; discussions fade into inconclusiveness; everyone leaves the table with assumptions intact and without the rude starkness of a closure.

By eleven, most guests have eaten, conversed awkwardly, and left. Having cleared the table, the workers begin to wash the pots and pans: Little Shawkat scours them with a coconut husk and abrasive ash before passing them to Altaf, who rinses them and lays them to dry. Before long the hotel manager appears at the kitchen door, a rare occurrence at this hour. Altaf and his associate stop their work and look up, puzzled.

"I am told that Farida Auntie didn't come for dinner today," the manager remarks, sounding concerned.

"No sir, she didn't," Altaf replies.

"Did her nephew eat?"

"Yes sir, he had dinner pretty early," interjects Little Shawkat. "I think he went out afterwards. He always goes for a smoke after dinner. But today he looked like he was in a rush."

The manager thinks for a few seconds. "I think something is wrong," he says pensively.

"If you want, sir, I can go and check," offers Altaf.

The manager looks at him with approval, as though that is exactly what he wanted to hear. He nods. "Yes, do that, and report back to me."

Altaf rinses his hands, wipes them quickly on the side of his trousers, and heads upstairs. He pauses in front of the guestroom, leaning forward to check if he can hear anything from inside. *Nothing. I'm sure she's just asleep.*

With trepidation, Altaf taps softly on the door.

A voice responds, weak but hopeful: "Is that you, Fazle?"

"No, Farida Auntie, this is Altaf."

The unexpected answer elicits a long pause, which Altaf feels compelled to break: "You have not eaten tonight, Auntie. Is everything all right?"

"I've been feeling dizzy," she says slowly. "Altaf, can you send some food to my room, something simple?"

"Yes. I will bring something up."

Altaf hastens back to the kitchen, prepares a plate of rice, greens, and fish, and after a quick detour to the manager's office to report on the activities, which seems to pacify the manager's anxiety, carries the tray up to Farida auntie's room, balancing it on his right hand while using his left to tap softly on the door. Asked to come inside, he finds her sitting on the bed, her figure imposing and unwieldy, accentuated with shadows in the dim yellow glow of a single light bulb hanging from the ceiling. The room is a mess. Her clothes are everywhere, sari-blouse-petticoats and *shelwar-kameez*, interspersed with fashion magazines and books to suit her state: Managing Your Pregnancy, 101 Proper Muslim Names for Boys, and others of that sort. He looks around to find space to set down the tray. The desk is covered with containers, of all sizes, shapes and colors: nail polish, perfume, lotions, sundry applicators. The small bedside table is a veritable dispensary, piled with bottles of syrups, elixirs, expectorants, and analgesics, tubes of ointments and balms, and scatterings of tablets and capsules. A bit baffled, he looks at her to receive guidance. "Just put down the tray on the bed," says Farida Auntie.

Altaf complies. Farida Auntie reaches for the plate, moving her hands delicately, ten fingers with ten manicured nails, painted golden to match the small gold rings on her ears.

"Where is Fazle?" She says under her breath, as though she is asking herself.

"He went out after dinner. I don't know where," replies Altaf. "Is there anything else I can get you?"

"That nephew of mine is unreliable," says Farida Auntie in a disapproving voice. "I am not doing well. It's not easy being in this state. But where is he when you need him? He's probably made friends at the tea-stall on the street and having a smoke with them. Oh, my misery." She shakes her head while mixing the rice with the greens. "And those cigarettes will kill him like they killed his father."

Altaf listens with a polite posture, his head slightly bowed, his eyes fixed on the floor.

"My husband is supposed to arrive tomorrow. I'll be so relieved when he's finally here."

"Where is he, Auntie?" Altaf asks softly.

"In Kuwait. He's coming tomorrow evening. Kuwait Airways 281. I've memorized the flight number. You know what I think? I think he'll come just in time to see his new baby boy. I've told him to bring soft clothes, shirts and half-pants. Oh and toys, too, and some delicious foreign food, and a velvet blanket. We'll soon have a wonderful little boy, *Inshallah*." The topic of these imminent arrivals, topped with savory morsels of fish-in-rice, seems to energize Farida Auntie, dispelling bit by bit the clouds and shadows that were hovering over her earlier.

"He likes bringing things for his family," she continues while eating. "The last time he visited—that was nine months ago—he brought back a huge machine called microwave. It's in our home, in Netrokona. We didn't have a place for it, so we put it on a table in the drawing room. It was so big that when our neighbors came in they thought we had a new tv!" Auntie chuckles. "I haven't used it. I don't want to damage the sheen. And most of the time, we don't have electricity anyway."

"He doesn't stay long when he visits?" inquires Altaf while pouring her a glass of water from a jug.

The gloom threatens to return across Auntie's face. "No." She sighs. "He has been working there from before we were married. He gets only one vacation a year. He says the Kuwaitis will fire you and cancel your visa if you ask for more. But he has managed to get special permission to visit early, before the year is over, you know, with my condition." A hint of smile appears on her red lips, lingering for a second before receding into a quiet solemnity as she pauses to think, beginning to look worried. "Oh, I hope it's not something else."

"What do you mean, Auntie?" Altaf asks, surprising himself with the promptness with which he posed the question.

"I hope he hasn't lost his job!" She shakes her head again after pondering the possibility. "It was hard for us the last time he lost his job. That was three years ago, in Qatar. He was working in construction and they sent him back. We were newly married then. I was so happy to have him back, but his mind was not with me. He was unhappy and angry most of the time. Still, I was hopeful. I kept telling him, forget about Qatar, you can work here. After a few months he found another manpower agent who was recruiting workers for Kuwait."

"I know men in our village who went to Saudi, Qatar, Kuwait and those places," Altaf remarks.

Farida Auntie does not seem interested. Finished with the rice, she begins to quietly grind a fish bone to suck its juices, before throwing it on a heap of chewed pulp on her plate. She pushes the plate away and gets up to wash her hands. "My husband says he has a better job now," she says absent-mindedly. "He sends more money every month for me and his father."

Altaf pours her another glass of water and begins to organize the tray. She returns from the washroom and clambers back on to the bed. "Anyway," she says, in the defined tone that marks a conclusion reached, "I think all these years he has spent in a foreign country will come to an end. It will, once he sees the sweet face of his new boy *Inshallah*."

Altaf catches himself on the verge of uttering something, perhaps a point about the event imminent in his own life, but restrains the impulse, as though recalling that his position permits to not share but only listen. What emits from him instead is a soft sigh, barely perceptible, which he masks quickly with a question: "Do you need anything else, Auntie?"

"No. If you see Fazle, tell him to not disturb me. I am going to sleep."

Tray in hand, Altaf returns quietly to the kitchen. He sets it aside, and unbuttons his shirt, which went through, as it does every day, several rounds of sweating and drying, each a marker of a phase accomplished in the whirlwind that constitutes his day. He takes out the envelope Nani gave him earlier and opens it carefully to count the bills. *One thousand taka; unexpectedly generous.*

Altaf sits down on his favorite kitchen stool, listening to the faint ringing of the few crickets that linger past midnight. He opens one of the drawers in a cabinet and takes out a black notebook, its cardboard top threadbare from years of use. The thin ruled pages contain no writing; they merely serve as dividers of a makeshift album. Nestled between them are yellowed clippings from newspapers: a story about a festival near his village years ago, a report of a concrete school building being erected, an old advertisement for labor needed in a hospital in Saudi Arabia—kitchen staff, cleaners, drivers, and loaders whose benefit package is centered on "full uniforms provided." He flips through the pages idly until he finds a photograph, a black-and-white shot of two tired faces, as though they were forced to pose. He outlines with his finger the shape of the woman pictured, stopping at the infant on her lap. The little girl, wrapped in a patterned *kantha*, is just a few days old, yet she is looking straight at the camera. Leaning forward, he stares at her intently.

"Ma," he whispers. "A few more hours, ma."

Sunrise wakes Altaf from a night made fitful by the anticipation of seeing his family. He packs his bags energetically, but quietly; he wants to head out before anyone requests a morning chore. He has ways to go today. A city bus will take him to the long-distance terminal at Saidabad, where he will have to identify the call for his destination from the chaotic cries of conductors selling tickets to places around the country. After traveling three hours southeast on another bus, he will reach a *ghat* where fishing boats congregate, and with luck, spot someone going in the direction of his village.

By the time Altaf finds a boat, it is late afternoon. The boatman agrees to transport him, provided that they take a shortcut through rice paddies. The vast delta of Bengal has just begun its yearly cycle of floods. The paddies will be flooded and traversable by boat. Rivers will swell further over the next two months, inundating entire districts at a time, until only railroad tracks and roads built on earthen levees remain visible, along with treetops and occasional buildings standing on concrete stilts. The water will start to recede in autumn, leaving in its wake cesspools of mosquitoes and parasites. But for now it brings life, not death, and its rippling expanse invigorates Altaf as he sits on the deck, filling his lungs with moist air. The boatman and his son, a boy of twelve, wield light paddles to pilot the vessel up to the paddies, at which point Altaf gets up and joins hands with them. Delicate green sprouts break the grey surface of the water, but the submerged stems of the paddies are thick and strong, nourished by fresh silt. Neither oars nor motors are effective here. The crew and the passenger, working in unison, plunge a heavy pole into the water until one end of it wedges against the bottom. The boatman cries "push," and they pressure it with brute muscular force, pivoting it back and propelling the boat forward. When the boatman cries "lift," they yank the pole out of the underwater field, which seems unyielding like quicksand. They aim several yards ahead and plunge the pole again, repeating the process to the rhythm of the boatman's enthusiastic commands. Altaf works silently, happy that each stroke, however strenuous, brings him closer to home.

He reaches the village well after dark, a cluster of huts on high ground that usually stays above the flood level. With gentle moonlight illuminating the way, he walks along a path through bamboo groves, a path he used to take as a boy to go to school, by his grandfather's small pond that his father had sold a long time ago, past old hibiscus bushes still exploding with red and orange, and arrives at his doorstep exhausted and anxious but with the reassuring serenity of having returned to the familiar. He takes a deep breath and enters his tiny two-room house. His earnings over the years have upgraded its walls to corrugated tin, but the floor remains original, made of baked mud and covered by thin wicker mats that feel cool to the touch. The roof is also of corrugated tin, slanted, with a green wooden beam in the middle.

Altaf finds his brother in the sitting room. They smile and hug.

"How are things?" asks Altaf.

"Things are good, *Mashallah*," says Mizan, his brother. "I am so glad you're here."

"Altaf, is that you?" A tender female voice drifts from the room next door.

"*Bhabi* is in the other room. Go see her," says Mizan, extending his hand to point to the doorway over which hangs a thin cotton curtain.

Altaf parts the curtain and enters the bedroom. His wife, laying on a small old platform bed, turns to offer a tired gaze. "You've come just in time," she says. Another woman in a dark sari is standing near her, soaking a napkin in a bucket of water. Altaf recognizes her as the village nurse, that title a result of once having worked, for a few weeks, as an assistant to a mobile public health team that visited the region. He kneels in front of the bed and takes his wife's hand.

"How are you feeling, Kulsum?" he asks softly.

"You've come just in time," she repeats.

"It took me all day to get here."

"I don't want anything bad to happen. Someone wicked put a spell on us the last time. Who could it be, Altaf? Who hates us so much?"

"I don't know."

"How many days did our little ma live? Do you remember?"

"Kulsum, don't think about that," says Altaf. "It's not good for you to worry."

"I can't forget."

"Allah is giving us another chance."

Kulsum weeps silently as Altaf holds her hand. He thinks of another night a year and a half ago, a memory so happy and sad that it is no longer vivid; the faces are blurry even though he knows whose they are. He remembers wide-awake anticipation through screams of pain; he remembers pails of warm water, the sound of wet cloths being wrung, the murmur of relatives gathered outside and praying with their palms raised. He remembers relief, at last, at the labored cry of a baby, a wholesome, unmitigated, overpowering sense of relief. There were showers of *Mashallahs* and *Al-Hamdulillahs*, as though everyone's prayers had been answered. Kulsum recovered within a week. Altaf shuttled happily between the village and the nearby town to get supplies. It was winter, a season more conducive to travel, with no need for boats. It was during one of those trips to town that he ran into an old friend, the owner of a photo studio, who offered to take a set of pictures of the new family. Kulsum had never been photographed before; she was nervous. Altaf persuaded her, and they hired a rickshaw and went to town, took a few pictures in black-and-white, had sweets, and shopped for their baby. Altaf remembers, as his eyes well up with tears. *Two weeks. Our little ma lived for two weeks.*

Altaf touches his wife's cheek lightly. He remembers how shattered their world became after the loss. Life reversed so quickly from bliss to misery. In her delirium, Kulsum was convinced that taking the pictures had put a curse on the child: a baby that young should not have been exposed to a world of evil eyes. In his frenzy, Altaf tore all the photos, but stopped at the last, the one in which his little ma seemed to stare straight at him. He could not bring himself to erase the memory of her innocent face. He folded the photo in half and put it in his pocket, away from Kulsum's sight. With help and wisdom from the elders, they pulled through eventually—to the limited extent that inconsolable parents can—but Altaf felt that Kulsum blamed him, even though she never leveled an explicit accusation. There was nothing much to say anyway, and time was running out. Altaf had to return to work. Everyone back at Airport Hotel greeted him with felicitations, but he conveyed nothing in return except a vacant stare before averting his weary eyes. Nani understood right away. She caressed his face with silent affection when he went to the roof to bring her afternoon tea. She wanted to give him an extended leave, but he declined. No other word was spoken about what had happened. He immersed himself in work, with a strange politeness and hushed diligence that were perhaps the only expressions for his anguish. He began to send a greater part of his wages to his wife, once a month, addressed care of his brother Mizan. Yes, he remembers it all, but he does not want to.

Altaf looks tenderly at his wife again, and with a heavy sigh releases his hand from her clasp. "I will be back, Kulsum," he says. "I have to arrange some things."

She looks away without reply. He gets up, glances at the other woman, and quietly leaves the room.

Mizan was waiting outside, smoking a *bidi*. He quickly tosses it behind the bushes when he hears his brother approach the door.

"I think it will happen tonight," says Altaf.

"We're ready," says Mizan. "I've made all the contacts. They will light the fire as soon as we give them the news."

"Is it far?"

"No. It's close to the school. We can walk there in ten minutes."

"Do the elders know?"

"Yes. I think some of them are there already."

"Does Kulsum know?"

"I haven't told her. I don't think she has heard about it from anyone else."

Altaf stares quietly into the night.

"You should eat something," says Mizan. "Rashida Apa has prepared a meal for us."

"All right," says Altaf. He thinks for some time, then turns and looks at Mizan. "I will not lose another one."

"You will not, brother," replies Mizan, touching Altaf's arm.

They walk in silence to a neighbor's house where a warm meal awaits, and return promptly after a quick dinner. Altaf goes back into the bedroom where two other women have arrived to help. He exchanges silent nods with them, and sits by Kulsum's side for almost an hour. Then the labor begins. Altaf is asked to wait outside. A few neighbors gather; they reassure him and together they pace and pray as another hour goes by before Kulsum's wrenching voice and the busy shuffling of the midwives are consummated, and the adoringly young cry of a newborn is heard. Altaf and Mizan rush to the room to find a little baby daughter being delivered to the arms of an exhausted, expectant mother.

"All is well," says the nurse-midwife, smiling.

"Go!" exclaims Altaf, turning to Mizan, who nods knowingly and runs out.

"*Al-Hamdulillah*," Altaf mutters as he approaches Kulsum. He touches the baby's forehead.

His wife looks at him, and Altaf sees a blissful contentment unfolding across her usually pensive face. He gazes at her fondly, freely, but only for a moment, before struggling to suppress his emotion with an affected determination. "Let me take her," he says.

With delicate grace, Kulsum yields the child into Altaf's arms. He stands up, his eyes fixed on his daughter. "I need to free her," he says in a gritty voice. He turns around and walks out with the baby.

"Where are you going?" cries Kulsum, as the other women in the room converge on her to gently pin her down. "Where is he taking my baby?" she asks them repeatedly, writhing in vain to break free as her words become mingled with frantic sobs.

With the infant in his arms and the neighbors following him, Altaf walks on, past those hibiscus bushes, past his ancestor's pond, unperturbed as the anguished pleadings of his wife fade across the thick bamboo groves. They leave the village and march along narrow uneven paths that demarcate the crop fields until they reach a large clearing surrounded by coconut trees, awash in moonlight. Dozens of villagers, old and young, are gathered there. A fire is aglow in one corner, being fed branches and dry leaves by some boys. Mizan, who was waiting with the group, rushes out to greet Altaf.

"All the elders are here!" exclaims Mizan.

Altaf nods and walks straight into the congregation. He is accosted by an old man with telltale marks of piety: an attire of white *punjabi-pajama* and a white cotton cap, a face inundated in white beard, and in the middle of the forehead a dark spot created by a lifetime routine of prostrate supplication before God. *On the Day of Judgment, the brow of the faithful will shine, and all will witness those with merit separated from the idle and the sinners.* Altaf recalls a frequent sermon at the mosque where his father used to take him on Fridays.

The pious old man proceeds to inspect the baby, running his fingers from her head to toe. "We have a healthy child," he proclaims, a testimony acknowledged at once by the crowd with a satisfied collective hum.

Altaf feels the eyes of the crowd upon him and his child. A chill runs down his spine. "You are the child's father," says the old man, turning to Altaf and sensing his apprehension. "You have done the right thing. The *ojha* is ready. Be brave and hold her firmly."

Altaf's muscles tighten as another man with long scruffy hair, naked except a white cloth wrapped around the waist, draws closer, his gait uneven, his eyes dilated and roving, his thin arms dangling loosely by his side.

"Ha!" cries the man. "You will do as I say." He jerks out a needle from his cloth, and with a singular leap arrives right in front of Altaf, pinches the baby's earlobe with his dirty fingers, and pierces it. The baby yelps in her tiny voice. Altaf's arms begin to shake but he concentrates on keeping his stance firmly on the ground.

"I have the prescription that you need, child," shouts the *ojha*, the village shaman. "I will deliver you from the ills that you get from your mother. I will fight your misfortune. I will defeat the demons that want to haunt you in birth and in death." He laughs. "You," he says, focusing now on Altaf, "you will do as I say. Raise your child high, as high as you can."

Altaf obeys. The *ojha* shakes and hops, and raising his hands, cries out, "Come now, you vile spirits, come and snatch this girl away if you dare." Altaf holds his baby aloft. She is terrified in his arms, her instinctive infant protests too feeble against the shaman's raucous barks.

By now the fire that was set has been fanned to a great height. The witch-doctor prances around the blaze, his lips fluttering with strange incantations. His disciples, bare-chested and long-haired, chant along, goading him to an uncontrollable fervor. The flames leap up, casting crackling sparks all around.

"Where's the blacksmith?" shouts the witch-doctor.

The village blacksmith walks up in a hunched, submissive posture, and offers what he was summoned to bring for the ritual.

The *ojha* looks at the iron rod, and nods his consent. He shakes it as if to check if it was solid. He waves the rod above his head and flings it at his pupils. He closes his eyes and begins to chant again. An apprentice picks up the rod and blesses it with some secretive magic. It is put into the raging fire and heated till it becomes a gleaming red.

The singing stops.

"Make way for the *ojha*, come on now, move, make way," cry the disciples. The witch-doctor carries the radiant rod like a lance, walking steadily toward the little girl. A death-like lull falls over the crowd. Everyone fears sorcery. Boys try to push their way to the front and make noise, only to be firmly hushed by their parents. The *ojha* stops in front of the frightened baby. He holds the rod just inches from her face. Then he lowers it.

The little girl squirms and screams and whimpers and screams again till she can cry no more. She tries her best to get herself loose, throwing her little arms and legs, but Altaf holds her strongly while the shaman works on her. Her small, young forehead is scorched with the sinister wand; the sizzle and stench of newly-born charred flesh causes every mother in the crowd to shut their eyes and shudder. A solid black mark is burnt between her eyes, a permanent stamp to keep the spirits away.

"I have given her a third eye," declares the *ojha*, "to remain vigilant even when she's asleep, and no *jin-pori* and wicked spirit will ever harm her."

Altaf still holds her high, serene and composed.

Felicitations once again greet Altaf on his return to Airport Hotel, and the beaming father responds with warm handshakes and hugs. With minimal chores assigned to him that day, he prepares an elaborate tray of afternoon snacks, including his signature spicy *samosas* and chutney, and carries it to the roof. As Nani samples the treats and sips her cup of tea with anticipation, sitting back on her wicker chair, Altaf proceeds to update her, with evident satisfaction, on what transpired during his visit home and the considered measures he took to ensure for his daughter a childhood free of jinx, only to find, to his astonishment, that his story has infuriated his initially affectionate audience.

"Stupid, stupid fool!" Nani roars before Altaf could finish. Trembling, she gets up from her seat while trying to support her fragile body on the cane. "This is the twenty-first century. How can you be such a monster, such an idiot?" She shakes her head violently and turns to Little Shawkat, "Can you believe this?"

"Please calm down, Nani," implores Little Shawkat, extending his arms to steady her, afraid that she may fall.

Nani is not pacified easily. "You should be whipped," she screams at Altaf, panting. "Get out of here, you satanic father. How could you do this?"

Altaf stands still, polite as usual, his head bowed down.

"Do you know you have made her life hell?" cries Nani, beginning to attract other hotel workers nearby. "Have you thought, you inconsiderate fool, how you will ever marry her off to a decent man with a scar like that fixed right on her face?"

Altaf stands in submission while she continues her outburst, shifting erratically between rage and reason. Then, out of exhaustion more than the entreaties of her attendants, she lets her body slump down to her chair, and her shouts subside into a fuming silence. "Tell him to leave my sight," she says. With dejection and remorse etched on his face, Altaf walks away.

Later that night, upon advice from Little Shawkat, Altaf approaches Nani again. He tiptoes to her bed and stands next to it, nervous and unable to utter anything. She turns on her side, glances at him, and then turns away, clasping her side pillow.

"Nani, would you like some water?" he asks softly.

She does not reply. He waits for a minute, and sits down, cross-legged, on the floor next to her.

"That Farida Auntie also gave birth while you were gone," says Nani, her voice betraying a quiet exasperation. "It happened two days after her husband arrived."

"Here?" asks Altaf.

"It wasn't here. They went to a hospital. She needed an operation, Caesarian." Nani pauses to catch her breath before continuing: "They really wanted a boy. After the operation, when the doctor brought them a healthy beautiful girl instead, Farida went into shock. She wanted to deny the fact so much that she was convulsing. She had to be put on oxygen and some drugs. Her husband didn't speak to her for a long time. I had sent one of the maids with her, just in case, and that's how I heard."

Altaf listens quietly.

Nani turns around and looks at him from inside her mosquito-net. "Even *my* son was like that," she murmurs. "He had three girls, but he wasn't happy until finally he had a boy. Other people talked. I could see them struggling to keep it to themselves. When they felt they would burst if they had to keep it anymore, someone would come forward to him and say, 'I am sorry that another girl has been born to you; I wish you better luck next time.'" Nani sighs. "A girl is a mother. How can you be sorry that a mother is born?"

the price

2011
MARCH

Amin's mother was worried. After three days of rain and just a few hours' respite, the monsoon clouds had begun to gather again. She thought she had time. She was dusting around her hut at leisure—not that she had many belongings to care for, but the act of cleaning and picking comforted her. She opened the windows, with caution, for the wood was worn out from years of pelting by the elements. She tied a clothesline across the veranda and hung a few of her son's shirts that she had washed, knowing that the damp air would be unkind. She nodded to neighbors who, too, were busy with similar chores. Dry spells were rare at this time of the year. The motions of life had to be injected with hope and condensed to fit whatever breaks the weather offered. Who knew how long this break would last.

Soon enough, the daylight inside the hut darkened. Shadows lost their form. Amin's mother interrupted her work and looked outside, and saw the afternoon sun withdraw behind a mass of gray that had begun to swirl and heap upon itself in thick layers. "Oh god," she muttered. "I have to get to the bazaar." From an old Nabisco tin that once contained biscuits and now her valuables—a bangle or two and some cash—she pulled out the bills she could find. She folded them into a bundle and secured it with a knot into her sari. She wound the sari tightly across her waist, and, snatching a jute bag from a door-side hook, hurried out.

A squiggly dirt path led to the market half a mile away. Amin's mother walked fast. The earth, saturated, was soft under her feet; it kneaded her heels as she strode. Her gait was steady and she looked straight. Yet she knew the subtleties around her. She knew that if she turned right she would see the levee in the distance, on which the silhouette of villagers looked funny, like ants. Beyond the levee ran a river, angry and bloated with rain. On her left, a grain field swayed in gentle waves. She knew its rhythm: always more tender than that of the waters. A tiny smile softened her cheeks, as she remembered playing in the undergrowth when she was young. The field was flanked by a banana orchard, and if she were to look that way, she would see cows rambling back home on their own. She knew that the anxious bleating of Shakur's goats, tied to a tree, would soon come within earshot. That boy was always late to shepherd his animals to safety. Amin's mother walked—and though she was focused on the task ahead, she enjoyed distractions that pranced in the margins of her consciousness. She knew this land. She knew its stories and its creatures—most of them anyhow.

She could now see the bazaar. In flat terrain anything placed reasonably high could be seen from a distance. If local traders had their way, they would have set up the bazaar on the levee, visible far afield. But the levee was off-limits by consensus. It was earthen and fragile, and breaches in it would mean disaster in the rainy season. So, commerce resorted to the second-highest point. The market was set up on a bridge. It spanned a narrow canal fed by the river. Amin's mother remembered when the bridge was laid. She was ten or eleven, and she and her friends had skipped school to attend the ground-breaking ceremony. They watched a political dignitary arrive with fanfare. They made faces to each other as he delivered a droning speech. He stood with his belly out, shoulders tucked in, and hands clasped on his lower back, as if he had just swallowed a giant pear. She had seen that awkward posture on other city folk, who came to her village occasionally to inspect things like community clinics or tube-wells. After the speech and the customary slogans were over, promising to transform the country and death or worse to its enemies, the man was brought a pick, with a ribbon tied to its handle. His body shook as he lifted it. She and her friends laughed and laughed as his thin arms, seldom to suffer physical labor, tried to thrust the blade into the moist soil. His deputies made light of the affair and led a round of clapping. She did not understand why they cheered when he had clearly failed. She could not think of any situation in which she was praised after falling short—whether it was separating husk from grain, or carrying a vat of water on her head, or fanning cinder with bellows, which had burnt her fingers. People from the cities, they did everything differently. They stepped in to give their leader a hand, a rescue that he hailed as an example of the friendly ways of his government. Everybody clapped again. She and her friends did too, and since that day they visited the site often to watch masons at work. They played around, and sometimes brought the workers guavas they had stolen from neighbors' trees. The foundation was dug, the abutments went up on the two banks, and then came the monsoon. The work had to be stopped. For four months, the two concreted sides protruded through the mud like monuments erected to the rain gods. The masons returned at last and laid a deck over the culvert, high enough to allow fishing boats to pass under it. Young men from the villages came with shovels and baskets, itching to make themselves useful. They stuffed dirt and mud to raise the earthen ramp so that it met the deck. The bridge was ready. But the locals had to wait until the dignitaries again descended from the capital, unveiled a plaque to dedicate the bridge, and raised their hands to pray for prosperity, failing which, for God's forgiveness. She and her friends, dressed in their best clothes, went through the motions too, lining up, praying, and cheering. What they really wanted to do is run across their new bridge. But they had to wait, and wait. The dignitaries crossed first, stopping here and there to push against the parapet to see if it was strong, to caress the plaster to see if it was smooth. Then marched the city officers and their bedecked wives. By the time the party workers came to cross, people had become impatient: they were rudely pushing and shoving to board rickshaws and buffalo carts. It would have been simpler to walk. But ceremonial walking did not attract the villagers, who walk all day; they wanted to be conveyed over their bridge and they were ready to pay cash for it. Rickshaw-pullers, dripping sweat, toiled to pull entire families, implausibly piled three-layers high in the small carriage: the parents rooted in the seat, with infants entrenched in lap, and toddlers and teenagers branched out precariously on the sliver of cushion on top of the backrest. The weight of such enthusiasm was considerable, and before long the tread of the rickshaws, the squeaky wheels of the carts, and the hefty hooves of the bullock began to unsettle the earth. The bridge stood solid, of course, but the earthen ramp slipped, and the step up to the deck became too high for wheeled traffic. In came the young men with their shovels and baskets to pack dirt into the ramps. People waited, the road was raised, vehicles passed, the road slipped again, and the men packed it again. It was a joyous affair. Amin's mother sighed and her shiny black eyes narrowed with a smile. That cycle continues, she thought. The earth erodes and people step in to care for it.

Close to the bridge now, she saw a new layer of mud on the ramp, pressed and rolled smooth. That was expected: these days the maintenance cycle coincided with the market. The young men with shovels were no longer volunteers; they had become workers paid by the merchants for upkeep. A few of these workers lingered about, smoking and chatting. Not many traders were in sight. Amin's mother admonished herself: instead of cleaning around the house, she should have left sooner. The market did not run on a set schedule. One just had a gut feeling that a given day would be market day. Sellers and buyers got together as if driven by a collective instinct, and the winds then carried the buzz into the villages to bring everyone out. No guesswork was necessary today. After all that rain, the market was a certainty. What Amin's mother was unsure about was whether she would be able to find the ingredients she needed. She wanted her son to come home to a sumptuous hot meal.

Veiled flashes of lightning somewhere in the sky let out grumbles from the clouds. Amin's mother looked up, alarmed. "Please don't start to rain yet," she pleaded while, inaudibly, still chiding herself. Speeding up the gentle slope of the ramp, she passed farmers heading back with baskets on their head. Empty steel canisters, earlier filled with fresh milk or hot tea, dangled from some shoulders. The few traders left on the bridge were busy packing. Amin's mother had seldom seen the bridge so empty, so quiet. On a good sunny day, the road would be baked hard and the concrete slab would rest solid, suspending a noisy crowd above the canal. Town-merchants would come to retail their wares: bright rubber sandals, trinkets inlaid with Koranic verses, kerosene, everyday medicine. Smaller traders would lay their wicker baskets and squat on both sides of the road. Their haggles and quibbles would give off an intimate energy, the happiness of offering one's harvest to others. Everyone ended with a decent bargain. Today the vigor was absent and the colors seemed dull. The sellers that remained had covered their baskets with plastic sheets that reflected the gray clouds overhead.

Amin's mother approached a bearded farmer who was talking to a boy she knew, one of Amin's friends whose name she could not remember. They seemed agitated. She slowed her walk, and listened in.

"Twenty people?" asked the farmer.

"Yes, all were put in a single van," said the boy.

"My God," said the farmer.

The boy saw Amin's mother and brought his conversation to an end. He gave her a salaam. She walked up, said nothing, and lowered her gaze to the vegetables in the farmer's basket: a few eggplants resting forlorn underneath a plastic sheet. She picked the one with the tautest skin and fewest spots. "How much?" she asked.

"Eight taka, usually." replied the farmer. "But just five will do. I've got to wrap up and go."

"Everyone's leaving so soon," said Amin's mother.

"There weren't many people today."

"Oh?" Amin's mother asked inattentively as she placed the eggplant in her bag.

"They were scared," interjected the boy.

"Yes, the weather's been bad," Amin's mother said. She handed the farmer five taka.

"It's not the rain," said the boy. "They were scared of the police."

Amin's mother glanced at him, a touch of anxiety unfolding across her face.

The boy dropped his voice and said, "A big police team raided the town yesterday because of the price crisis."

That sounded familiar. "I think I heard that," she said, recalling that the morning news on her neighbor's radio had delivered that phrase with some concern. She could not remember the context.

"Mahbub here has just returned from town," said the farmer, pointing to the boy.

Amin's mother looked at Mahbub. "My son works in the town," she said in a pensive tone. "Have you seen him?"

Mahbub averted the gaze. "No, I haven't," he said. "But I'm sure he's doing well."

"He's coming back tonight," said Amin's mother.

Mahbub stared at her for a moment. "That's great," he said softly. "I'll see him around then." He squinted, as though he had seen something in the distance. "I have to go. I should get home before it starts to rain."

"Keep me posted of any updates you hear," called out the farmer as Mahbub hurried away. "What's your son doing in town?" he asked Amin's mother.

"He has lined up some business. Contract work, I think."

"Oh, no problem then," said the man. "It's only us farmers that the police are after."

"Why are they after farmers?" asked Amin's mother.

The bearded man sighed and shook his head. "They're saying that *we* created this price crisis. They can't control the country. Prices are rising everywhere and people are starting to talk against them, so they're looking for someone to blame."

Amin's mother looked at the farmer for the first time. Trained to avoid eye-contact with unknown men, she had learnt to get more from less, and a quick glance was all she needed for a probing look. The man was incensed. "They're doing whatever they want," he growled. "I sell vegetables. I don't even make enough to buy seeds for next year. I have to bribe someone to get a government loan. And they come and tell us that *we're* corrupt and *we're* cheating the people. What's this country coming to?"

He glanced at the other end of the bridge. "They keep on sending their goons to harass us. Look, they're coming again."

Amin's mother turned and saw two men in uniform approaching from a distance, in watchful steps. One of them carried a gun.

"There is a crisis," whispered the farmer. "But they created it, not us."

The men walked towards them. Amin's mother did not move. Her hand sunk, by its own volition, into her jute bag and began to shift its contents around. Her gaze was on the farmer's basket, which lay at their feet and which he pretended to organize in unnecessary detail. The world outside seemed to close in, slowly blurring the landscape, removing the chatter of the marketplace. For a moment Amin's mother thought that the basket of eggplants was the only object that remained on the bridge, that the bridge itself had been amputated from society. Then her mind refocused, not on what was before her eyes nor on the bustle that kept her hands busy, but on what was occupying, gradually, a larger space in her peripheral senses: pressed uniforms, insignia and epaulets, the shiny black barrel of a lowered gun, its magazine, the trigger, a finger resting on alert behind it, and the steady beat of boots that seemed to rise louder, and louder, till it stopped, next to them.

"How much have you sold today, uncle?"

Amin's mother glanced at the soldier who hurled the question. He's Amin's age, she thought, in early twenties. He seemed uncomfortable, voicing an air of authority to stamp out a natural respect for an older man. Is he a constable or a border guard? Amin would have known. Amin would have even recognized the type of gun the soldier had. Amin! She could not complete her stream of thought. A wrenching emptiness crept out of her memories and began to radiate into the fullness of her mind. Amin, my boy! Why haven't you written? The last letter you wrote was two months ago. You didn't even go to get your father's pension this month. I've looked after what I can. I'm so happy I'll see you tonight. I am making your favorite meal, eggplant and fish with rice. God only knows what you've fed yourself the past two months. My son! Amin's mother trembled.

"Auntie, I am asking you a question."

Amin's mother stared vacantly at the soldier.

"Why are you shaking? Are you feeling all right?"

"Yes," she said. She straightened herself.

"Did this man charge you a fair price?" asked the soldier.

"Yes."

The soldier looked at her to see if she was telling the truth. He read her with a slow sweep from face to toe, registering her black eyes, the dark bronze skin of her hands, and her lithe body, now straight as a mahogany tree and draped in arcs of a cotton sari of a dim, depleted green. He said nothing. Amin's mother pulled her sari to cover more of her hair, a gesture of shy acknowledgement rehearsed since childhood.

“Good,” said the soldier in a tone of approval. “If you think you’re being over-charged by anyone, you should come and tell us right away. We want to make sure that people treat each other fairly.”

Amin’s mother nodded.

The soldier turned to the farmer with confidence, the discomfort of his relative youth now beaten back. He poked his gun into the basket, pulled aside the plastic cover with a deft swipe, and pointed the barrel to an eggplant. “Your vegetables are sickly,” he said with a snigger. He stood for a few seconds to enjoy his satisfaction with the proceedings, and then walked away with his colleague in tow.

Amin’s mother watched the soldiers recede from plain view. “I have to get some fish,” she said in a matter-of-fact tone. The farmer returned a glance that suggested goodbye, and Amin’s mother walked to the far end of the bridge. A tea stall stood on the earthen ramp, vacant of customers. Amin’s mother went around the back of the stall and climbed down the side of the ramp, stepping on brushes for traction and avoiding bare mud. She proceeded under the bridge to the water’s edge where a few fishermen, bare-chested and glistening, had moored their dinghy boats.

“What’s the catch today?” She asked a man atop the first boat.

The man replied with a smirk: “Well, how much have you got?”

She took out her bills. “Twenty taka.”

The man laughed. “You won’t get any real fish for that, sister. I told you last week. Better to save your money for rice and lentils.”

“I thought you might have some small fish. My son is coming tonight. I want to cook—”

“Yes, yes, I know,” the man interjected. “Try that last boat over there. They’re new. They might have small fish for you.”

How does he know about my son? Amin’s mother wondered as she went over to the last boat. A boy, barely twelve, sat on the deck, folding a net.

“Are you selling fish today?” Amin’s mother asked.

“Yes, but my father is not here,” said the boy without looking up.

"Where is he?"

"He went up to the bridge. Some policeman wanted to ask him something." The boy looked at Amin's mother and paused, realizing that his customer was not well-off. "What do you want?" he asked.

"I just want fish worth twenty taka."

"There's nothing below a hundred taka."

"Isn't there something, maybe something small?"

The boy shook his head and went back to folding the net. Amin's mother stood there, unsure of what to do. She looked downstream, all the way toward the levee, beyond which lay the river. She imagined how ferocious its swells must be now, for even the narrow canal by which she stood seemed electrified with eddies and ripples. The moored boats bobbed up and down; their wood croaked and their ropes squealed. She looked at the boy again, who was now bailing water out of the hull with a bucket. Nobody seemed idle, yet few got paid. She herself had little left to spend. If Amin did not send money soon, she would have to turn to her neighbors for help, again. And how long could she keep up the pretense, sending her son to collect the measly pension of a husband long dead? Somebody was bound to tell on them, sooner or later. And why is fish so expensive when there is so much water around?

Just about then Amin's mother spotted two large aluminum tubs on the shore, next to the boat. Fishermen usually filled these with water to store their catch. The lids were ajar. That was a good sign: it meant there was fish inside. Amin's mother glanced at the boy: he had moved on to another task, which she could not see, for he had his back toward her. She only heard a dull, rhythmic knock; perhaps he was hammering something? This was an opportunity. If she moved carefully, she could probably make off with a fish or two. She was surprised at the ease with which the idea consumed her thoughts, driving out the guilt she had felt at its arrival. She looked around. Satisfied that nobody was paying attention, she walked to a container and slowly lifted its cover. A noxious whiff of fish and slush seeped out; she winced. Her fingers quivered, and she tried to force them still, for the lid was thin, like a cymbal, and the slightest gaffe would betray her with a loud clang. Her throat dried, and the dews of sweat that formed on her forehead felt thick and heavy. With one hand she held up the lid, securing a gap just wide enough to sneak in the other hand. She could not see what was inside, nor did she intend to; instead her eyes darted between the boatmen chatting nearby. She only wished that the fish were small enough for her to grab and that the fins were not sharp. She dipped her hand into the water. Two or three scaly creatures slithered against her palm. What were they? She hoped they were not catfish or koi; those would be hard to catch unseen without risking a cut. Something almost bit her. She closed her eyes and tried to relax her hand. She felt a sloshing, and she clasped her fingers around whatever it was.

The grip was timed perfectly, such that her palm held up the creature's belly, her fingers arrested its wriggling, and her thumb avoided its dorsal fin. She took it out. It was a small snakehead murrel. It'd go well with eggplant. She tried to replace the lid, but could not bring herself to it. Her body was shaking. She realized that she was on edge, overcome with a sense of vulnerability: should anybody see her now, the prize in her hand would implicate her beyond doubt. How could she attempt such a caper, knowing that the police are patrolling the market right above? What a harebrained thing to do! They would surely throw her into their dreadful prison van, and then—. She could not imagine the consequences. Her heart pounded, and she thought that every beat must be audible to all on the bridge, booming above the thumps of that boy's hammer. But— she held her breath and listened in. She could not hear the hammer. She looked up, and froze.

The boy stood on the deck, staring straight at her.

Her world stopped. Her body no longer shook. On her right temple she sensed a pulse, which told her that she was conscious, but she knew that she had turned into a lump of flesh, unable to move, bent halfway over the tub with the lid in one hand and a squirming fish in the other.

"Abba," the boy called. He glanced past her, and raised his voice. "Abba, come quickly!"

A middle-aged man appeared, wearing a *lungi* and a white prayer cap. A mat of short white hair prickled out of his bare chest.

Amin's mother felt her wits return, forced by an aching back. She put the lid down and straightened her body.

"What is it?" asked the man, puzzled at the spectacle before him.

The boy said nothing. His gaze was locked with hers.

"What's going on?" asked the fisherman again.

"This woman," began the boy, speaking softly. "She wants to buy that fish."

The man barked: "You're not supposed to sell anything!"

"I told her she can have it for twenty taka," said the boy.

"What?"

"It's a small fish, so I told her it's twenty taka."

The man frowned and gauged his son. He thought for a few moments, moments that seemed to linger on, and then turned to Amin's mother. Pinching his lips, he said: "If that stupid boy has sold it to you already, I can't take it back."

Amin's mother was confused. She felt that she was floating above the scene, next to the bridge, watching below a figure in a green sari, around which a fisherman and a boy were going about their daily business. A father was coaching the skills of livelihood to his son, the same way that his predecessor must have taught him when he was young. Their boat looked old. It would surely struggle to survive another rainy season. Amin's mother felt sorry for the family, and she suspected that in a vague way she was responsible, but she could not deduce how.

In the meantime, that figure in the sari completed a transaction. A fish was placed in a jute bag, money was handed over, counted, and put away. No word was spoken. The figure walked slowly to the side of the bridge, and climbed up, getting closer with each step, until it was so close that its breathing could be heard, its nerves could be sensed, its sight could be perceived.

Amin's mother stood on the bridge, one hand on the railing. The jute bag she carried, dark and wet, smelled like turbid water. The creature inside no longer struggled; only a periodic spasm protested its fate. The tea-stall at the ramp now had two customers. They sat on a bench facing away, and from the aroma of fried puri and bhaji that swirled around them, Amin's mother knew that they were eating. She could hear them chat between morsels.

"I don't know what to do."

Amin's mother recognized that voice. It was Mahbub, that friend of Amin who was speaking earlier with the farmer. That was strange, she thought; he was supposed to have left for home.

"Will she find out?" asked Mahbub's companion.

"She knows," said Mahbub. "I mean, we've tried to tell her. She won't listen."

"But you've never told her fully."

"I don't know if I can."

"These damn flies!" the shopkeeper interjected, with wild swats that hardly bothered the insects that buzzed about.

"Did she come to the market today?" Mahbub's friend asked.

Mahbub sighed. "Yes, she came, as usual. She doesn't miss market day. I ran into her and had to escape."

"Didn't you say anything?"

"Well, I said that I'll see her son around when he comes back."

Nobody spoke for some time. Then Mahbub's friend shook his head. "You didn't have to lie," he said.

"What can I do?" Mahbub sounded irritated. "It's been two weeks now. She still believes that that he's coming back home."

"Everything's fucked up. What does she do with the food she cooks for him?"

"Only Allah knows."

The two customers signaled for more puri, and ate quietly, with the shopkeeper on watch for flies. A minute or so passed, and then the shopkeeper asked abruptly: "Where's the body?"

"We tried to get it," said Mahbub. "The police said they didn't know anything about it. I think they'll only hand over the body if his mother comes to claim it. You know, we're not close relatives."

Silence, once again, except for swishes of the shopkeeper's arm. He began to put the plates away. "I hear different things," he said, passing his customers a small jug of water. "But what exactly happened that day?"

Mahbub rinsed his hands. "Well, it was like what happened in town yesterday—" he began to explain, but his voice faded. Amin's mother did not understand why. She had stood on the bridge all this time and listened, facing away except occasional glances at the tea-stall. She craned her neck for a better look. She saw fluttering lips and gesturing arms, but she heard nothing, nothing but a faint ringing in her ears, a tinny sound that drifted in and out from afar. Mahbub and his companions did not see her, and she did not step any closer. She wanted to float again, glide with the wind toward those reckless gossipers and tell them how wrong they were about everything. But she could not will it. She simply watched them talk, seated smug and comfortable on a wooden bench, shaking their legs with excitement as they shared stories that made no sound.

Then she felt the first drops of rain.

She turned away and started to walk, toward the dirt road that trailed off the bridge's end. The freshly damp soil released a sweet scent, a fusion of pheromones between land and water. Clouds hung low on the horizon. All was quiet. Nature had taken a deep breath, and was holding it. Any moment now the wind will roar, and with a violent swoosh stir up those sturdy leaves in the roadside trees. Then will begin the downpour, beating a loud, unrelenting chorus for two or three days, maybe four. Amin's mother tightened her sari, and walked. The earth caressed her feet, as gently as it always did in the wet season, and her thoughts began to trickle, like tears. One moment she wanted to be carried home, where she would be safe. She could gather the shirts on the clothesline, shut the windows, and light her stove. The next moment she wanted to stay on the bridge till the heavy clouds melted on her and washed her away.

dhaka ঢাকা

2011 ২০১১
APRIL 16 এপ্‌রলি ১৬

ঢাকা, ১৬ এপ্রিল, ২০১১

ঝড়ের আভাস: সূর্য্য আড়াল নিয়েছে, আকাশ অন্ধকার, বাতাস বন্ধপ্রায়।

ঝড়-পূর্বক মুহুর্তের রূপ আমার বরাবরই পছন্দ; সব দেশেই অনাবিল মনে দেখেছি সে রূপ। তবে এবারই উপলব্ধি করলাম গঙ্গা-পদ্মার বদ্বীপে, আমাদের জলবায়ূতে সে রূপের নিশ্চিতাকার।

SIGNS OF A TEMPEST: THE SUN slips behind a thickening wall of clouds, the sky dims, and the wind all but disappears.

I have always loved ominous beauty of the world in the moments just before a storm. In every country I've been in, I've felt the same quiet exhilaration watching that transformation unfold. In the Ganges–Padma delta, shaped by the unmistakable logic of moist climate, the experience carries a different weight, a deep sense of inevitability.

গ্রীষ্মের প্রথম সপ্তাহ। শেষ বিকেল। কালবৈশাখী আসছে। নিকষ কালো মেঘের আবরণে প্রকৃতি নিশ্চুপ।

দিনমান ব্যস্ত শত পাখির কাকলী হঠাত করে শেষ। চেয়ে আছি কৃষ্ণচূড়া গাছের দিকে, আমার দৃষ্টি তার পাতার উপর; ছোট্ট সেই পাতা, বাতাসের বিন্দুমাত্র সমর্থনেই যে পাতা কাঁপবে থর থর করে সেই ছোট পাতাও নিষ্কম্প। দশ মিনিট পেরিয়ে বিশ মিনিট পঁচিশে গড়ালো, নেই একটুকু হাওয়ার রেশ। নেই এক সলতে স্ফুলিঙ্গ।

এই নিস্তব্ধতার আসলেই কোনো তুলনা নেই। প্রকৃতির এই অপরূপ স্তব্ধতা, অশান্তির আশংকায় বিরাজমান সেই অকৃত্রিম শান্তি একাধারে অপার্থিব, আবার একেবারেই দেশজ, বাংলাদেশের একান্ত এক উপহার।

It is the first week of summer. Late afternoon. A nor'wester is on its way. Nature, sealed beneath a ceiling of dark clouds, has gone suddenly still.

The relentless chatter of hundreds of birds - alive only hours ago - has stopped without warning. I find myself watching the Delonix tree, my eyes fixed on its fiery leaves. These are leaves that usually quiver at the slightest breath of air, yet now they remain perfectly still. Ten minutes pass. Then twenty. Then twenty-five. There is no wind at all, not the faintest ripple, not a single sign of motion.

This silence is unlike any other. The stillness feels deliberate, almost composed. A rare calm suspended beneath the threat of disruption. It is both unsettling and deeply familiar, both uncanny and unmistakably local. This fragile, breath-held moment, surreal peace poised on the edge of upheaval, feels like a tranquil gift - one uniquely belonging to Bangladesh.

the wisteria of villa nettuno

2011

They came out of the third bend in the road—and gasped. In front, almost without warning, was the Mediterranean Sea, in ominous deep blue in the fading light of the day, its waves crashing angrily against the jagged coastline.

"Slow," whispered Gabi. She rolled down her window. A roar of air rushed in, moist and salty.

Paolo took his foot off the accelerator and downshifted into second gear. The road ahead snaked uphill, climbing hundreds of feet from the waterline.

"I can't go that fast anyway," he murmured.

They drove in their bright green Fiat Punto for half an hour without saying a word, hushed, as it were, by the severe beauty around them. They felt as though they had entered a world of clear realities, of grand truths wrought between the resolute mountainside and the hypnotic sea. Like a delicate ribbon, Highway SS-145 was fastened precariously on to the edges of that fierce world. It looked artificial and out of place; humanity's meddling hands had pushed it into an equation where it did not belong—and the guilt of that intrusion seemed to weigh down on them. Their car moved along, slowing as night fell.

Paolo broke the silence first. "I wish they had lights on this road," he said. It's getting harder to see."

Gabi remained quiet.

"Why are the guardrails so thin?" Paolo continued. "This little scrap of metal won't stop us from crossing over the shoulder."

"Just drive carefully," Gabi said, uttering her words in slight annoyance, as though Paolo's inquisitive reflections were unnecessary, for the answers were evident. "If there were lights, the sea wouldn't look so wonderful, would it?"

"I know," Paolo said. "It's just that it's going to be late by the time we get there. I didn't think we'd have slow down like this."

Paolo's tone betrayed frustration. He was hungry; their last meal was several hours ago when they left Pompeii. They had not had the best of time today; something was amiss, and even simple tasks like getting lunch seemed an exertion. Things were often amiss these days, Paolo thought. And now he was getting tired from the keen attention that the winding road demanded. His left hand was busy maneuvering the steering wheel; his right was on the gear knob. "I can't enjoy the scene all that much," he grumbled. "Tell me if you see a parking area. I want to stop and take some pictures before it gets completely dark."

Gabi glanced at him, and went back to looking out the side window. She was feeling nauseous. She looked out as far as she could, focusing her eyes on the horizon. The fresh air helped, but the bends in the road were just too many. The car was moving in many directions, careening sideways, slowing abruptly to negotiate a sharp turn, accelerating again to make up for lost time. Gabi did not want to say anything. She was loath to bringing up her motion sickness. Her friends would accommodate her, sure, but there was always something that would go with it—a barely audible sigh, an almost imperceptible blink, or a subtle stretch of their body that would register a silent irritation and make her feel like a handicap.

All the same, it was becoming unbearable. She shifted in her seat and turned slightly toward Paolo, a minor attempt to convey a message while keeping her pride intact. His brown eyes were steady on the road. The Fiat seemed to fit his size well: his five foot nine frame was set snug, in firm command of the two-door car. He wore an olive green shirt that matched the shadow of his stubbles, denim trousers, and a new pair of sneakers that she had bought for him for this trip. These were supposed to be walking sneakers—"really funky," she had noted; "too teenage-like?" he had asked. "Oh, thirty-somethings can wear these easily," she had said, laughing, "and you mister, you look like you're twenty-two." He had laughed too, crinkling his nose in that way that she adored, and replied with one of his silly comebacks: "Well, *you* look like you're twenty-two."

Gabi sighed. Slow down Paolo. She still did not want to say anything. These things should not have to be laid bare. Staying together for many months should have programmed her weaknesses and needs into her partner's brain waves, shouldn't it? No—she affirmed silently to herself—she would not utter a word. Maybe he knew she was uncomfortable, and was driving rough to irk her. Maybe in his mind it was a battle, to be won by forcing her to beg mercy. Oh, whatever it is, just slow down.

"You know, I'm enjoying driving on this highway," Paolo said, looking straight. "It's like one of those roads they show in old movies: action scene, car chase."

"There's a spot ahead on the right. Can you pull over there?" asked Gabi, pointing to a small parking area that overlooked the sea.

Paolo saw the spot. "Aren't some cars parked there? Yea look, it's full. But, hello" - Paolo paused - "what are they up to?"

Gabi inspected the cars as they passed. The windows were rolled up, but shadows moved inside. "I think I know what they're doing," Paolo said with a sly smile. "The windows are steamy."

They drove by a few more scenic overlooks, each filled with small cars parked head-in with people inside. "So, this is where the locals come for their trysts," Paolo remarked. "I would have come here too if I lived here."

"How much farther is it to Positano?" asked Gabi.

"I don't know, maybe another twenty miles.".

"Forty minutes?"

"At least, at this speed."

Forty interminable minutes. The high price of beauty, Gabi thought. Beauty comes at high price, Gabi thought. They had planned to get away for long, and it had taken much effort—visas, papers, travel insurance, queues, security checks, red-eye flight. They hoped that the thrill to explore a place together would ease the tension that was beginning to brew between them. Paolo had started a new job, a position he had wanted for long, and at a place where he was ready to settle. Gabi wanted to leave hers. She saw the relationship as an avenue to freer times, in a different location, doing something else but together. With innocent enthusiasm each tried to convert the other, then started to disagree, a little, then more—until they realized that their language and pretexts and subtexts were no longer so innocent. It was remarkable how the same word uttered between the same people could begin to connote meanings so different from the original. Gabi could not place what had changed. Was it that the breathless emotions of courtship had exaggerated the meaning of things when Gabi and Paolo had just begun to know each other? Or had familiarity stripped away the generous benefits of doubt that they had initially given each other, baring them eventually to an insipid gist? Even love, which used to be a certain positive, liberating and sublime, now seemed an obstacle, blocking their otherwise individual paths and forcing them awkwardly toward a common center. They each had thought about the problem, and each considered the possibility that perhaps they were reading into the relationship too much, acting and ruminating in excess when things were best left unmanaged. And so, pauses began to interrupt conversations that used to be fluid. The wishful enthusiasm of a year ago gave way to a pact of quiet acceptance and a litany of unspoken concessions. They were still in love, they believed, and at times happy, they felt, but—. Take a break and do something different, advised a friend. Get away from routine, rediscover each other, confirmed another: it was common knowledge that relationships need an occasional detox. The magazines, the books, they all attest to this truth, insisted a third confidante, a colleague at Gabi's work. Gabi was left no option but to concur. Yet another friend, well-traveled and cosmopolitan, then suggested Italy's Amalfi Coast as the ideal locale to mount a rescue of the relationship. It was away, but not out of the way, developed yet natural; the weather was warm and sensuous, and the Mediterranean food promised to exhilarate. The trick was to find a destination that would not strain the management of fundamentals—food, toilets, communication and the like—so that they are left ample energy to focus on each other. The Third World was out of the question. You want controlled discovery, not wanton adventure. With the Amalfi Coast identified as the answer, Gabi showed Paolo some pictures as she carefully proposed the getaway one night, and to her surprise, he seized upon the idea. He too had wanted a retreat. He became excited at the possibility of driving in that cinematic panorama, and was soon printing road maps for their trip. Now here they were, far from Boston, advancing toward a tiny Italian town nurtured by mountains and water—but what she felt was nausea and what she wanted was to stop.

"Hey!" Paolo exclaimed, braking suddenly. He stopped the car, and then started to back up.

"What are you doing?"

"I saw a spot."

Paolo drove into a small nook. "They don't have any signs for this overlook. It's empty."

"Paolo, I don't know if it's an official parking spot. It's more like a clearing."

"Oh it's fine. Come on."

They stepped out of the car and into a gentle breeze, cool and moist from the touch of the sea. Gabi closed her eyes and took a deep breath. She felt refreshed immediately. Mediterranean oxygen. Paolo walked forward, cautiously nearing the edge; it was quite a drop to the waters below. Gabi waited, filled her lungs with purity once again, and satisfied, walked up to him.

"The moon is lovely," she said. It was suspended in front of them, unusually radiant. Itss long reflection shimmered on the waves.

"It really is." Paolo said. They stood in silence.

"What's that scent?" Gabi asked after some time, taking another deep breath.

"I only smell the sea," said Paolo.

"No, there's something else, something sweet. It's faint. You don't smell it?"

Paolo shook his head: "No."

"I think it's some kind of flower. Do you see any flowers?"

Paolo looked to the left, scanning the landscape and the horizon. It was dark. The road curved and disappeared into the mountains, and came out again by the water, coiling through the fog toward a small golden glow.

"That must be the town," Paolo said.

"I hope so," said Gabi.

Paolo put his arm on Gabi's shoulder. His fingers played a light tarantella on the side of her neck.

"I'm ticklish," she said.

"You look nice in the moonlight," said he, enunciating the words with clumsiness, which drew a faint smile on her face. Her long brown hair fluttered, and she seemed content, standing at ease in linen capris and a silky shirt that traced the contours of her slender body. Her perfect bosom swelled as though in unison with the sea. She seemed of the elements, a complement to the surroundings with her decisively Mediterranean features: strong, arched brows over sparkling eyes, lips full and luscious, and smooth skin that glowed from the moisture in the air. Paolo had never met anyone who changed with the weather as she did. She was vulnerable, pale, and depressed in winter, confident, luminous, and sumptuous in warmth. She is irresistible right now, thought Paolo, feeling a tension extend down his body as he stared at her. He touched her cheek and kissed her earlobe, and brought the other hand to rest on the small of her back. He could almost feel her skin through her thin shirt.

"The fog's rolling in. We should try to get to town," said Gabi under her breath.

A year ago, Paolo would not have given second thought to Gabi's attempt to divert his focus. He would treat it as pretense, reflexive playful protests that present themselves in order to be won over. Her language was different now, and Paolo could not quite tell whether it was his interpretation that had become blurry or her words that had become direct. He hesitated before announcing a matter-of-fact agreement: "Yes, I guess we should go." He walked back to the car, turned on the interior light and began to study the road map.

Gabi waited outside for another minute before she returned. "I'm ready," she said, closing the car door. "I feel better."

Paolo looked up at her to say something, but did not.

After driving for another half-an-hour, they reached the town's outskirts. Small sea-view motels appeared, the facade of which rested on the roadside, and the back was supported on stilts angled into the cliffs, high above the waterline. Paolo was impressed. "It's hard enough to build a road here, and they've built motels?" he said. "The space is so narrow and rough. You have to give credit to the persistence of these people."

He glanced at Gabi, offering an expectant pause to which she did not respond. He continued. "It's all about tourism. Money cuts mountains. And one day they will step back and ask, what have we done?" He paused again as he maneuvered the car through a tight curve. "At least they put up these hotels here without flashy signs," he said. "Imagine neon here. That would have spoiled everything."

"Look at the town; it's amazing," Gabi remarked. A string of lights nestled on the edge of the mountain—that was their destination. The mountain was sheer; there was no valley or plateau that lent itself naturally to habitat. The town had to be created with deliberate intent and carved out of rocks with dogged effort. Its defenses were strong, an array of hairpin bends and sharp twists through which ferocious minibuses shot out, like cannonballs, with a shriek of their horns. Paolo cursed each of them as he zigzagged the car while Gabi held her head in her hands for ten interminable minutes, until the road finally straightened and swooped downhill right into the town center.

"We're there," said Paolo with relief.

"About time," Gabi said. "I'll look for our hotel."

It was almost ten at night. A few pedestrians strolled the sidewalk that hung over the cliffs. The town spread vertically, with the road dissecting it through the middle. Houses and shops, all closed, were arranged in rows that went either up or down from the main street, and were accessible only through steep stairs that served as the town's alleys and byways.

Gabi tried to read the signs on the doorways. "The address says Viale Pasitea, but I can't see any road names here."

"But this must be it. I don't think there's any other road in this place," replied Paolo, pulling the car over the sidewalk. A minibus honked and squeezed past them, then rushed along. "They're crazy, driving like that," said Paolo as he straightened the car back on to the street.

"That's why the guide book said not to drive in these parts," said Gabi.

"But I like driving here. And it's convenient. We can stop whenever we need. Imagine taking one of those buses. You would have been sick."

Gabi looked at him, with subtle approval, and then remarked softly: "Yes I would've been."

They drove along the main thoroughfare for another ten minutes without luck. The storefronts along the way became sparse, and then the streetlights ended.

"It looks like we're already leaving," Paolo said.

"I didn't see any signs for the hotel," said Gabi. "Did you notice that nothing was open? We should ask someone."

"Look!" Paolo said. He had seen a side street on the left. He turned without waiting for a response. The street winded and climbed up in sharp spurts, such that they could see the main road and the town center shrink rapidly below. They came to a roadblock. Orange cones and barriers were peppered around, and a few men loitered about, wearing hard hats.

"That's strange, working at this hour of the night," remarked Paolo.

"Let's ask them about the hotel." said Gabi.

Paolo pulled up as Gabi rolled down her window. A portly man walked over and took a good look at them. "You cannot go more," he said in accented English, having determined that the occupants of the car were foreign. "The road is closed. Rock falling from the mountain."

"Sorry, but we're looking for a hotel," Gabi said. "It's called Villa Nettuno. Do you know where it is?"

"Villa Nettuno?" The man hesitated. "Villa Nettuno … You wait, I ask," he said, and walked back to the other workmen. They discussed the hotel's whereabouts with animated gestures, and pointed in different directions before before they settled on a consensus. The man returned with the verdict. "Yes, Villa Nettuno. I know. You go to main road. Go inside town, seven hundred meters. Then look on right side, you look for small sign."

"Oh, we left it behind then," Paolo said, sounding relieved.

Gabi smiled at the man. "Thank you," she said.

The man did not smile back. He just stood by, looking uncomfortable. After a glance back at his friends, he bent closer to Gabi and Paolo, and lowering his voice, uttered slowly: "Be careful."

Gabi looked at him, puzzled. Without reply, Paolo put the car in reverse and turned it around. They went back the way they had come, down the moonlit hill toward the intersection with the main road.

"Seven hundred meters," Paolo said after they had reached the main road.

"What did he mean, 'Be careful'?" Gabi asked.

"I think he was telling us to watch out for rockslides," said Paolo. His voice seemed affected, and shallow, and Gabi did not seem convinced by the explanation. He realized her unease but did not elaborate further, and concentrated instead on watching the odometer, providing Gabi with loud readouts every hundred meters while Gabi looked for the hotel. They saw it right around the seven hundred meter mark: a little green sign with cursive gold lettering, hung inconspicuously over a knee-high small wrought-iron gate. A light glowed behind it, and they saw that the gate was at the foot of a staircase leading up.

"Should I drop you off and look for parking?" asked Paolo.

Gabi hesitated, and Paolo offered a revised suggestion. "Look, I can't come with you and leave the car blocking the street. I'll wait here while you go and check if anyone is awake."

"Okay," said Gabi. She got out and walked toward the gate. She gave it a tentative push, and it creaked open. Signaling to Paolo that she was going inside, she walked up the stairs, and disappeared around the corner. A few minutes passed. Paolo began to feel a tinge of worry. He should have ventured inside, he thought. Gabi could have waited with the car, and if it had obstructed traffic—which would be unlikely seeing that the town had gone to sleep already—she could have honked and he would have come back. With the uneasy sensation that a mistake had been made, Paolo stepped out of the car and looked up. Only a small part of the hotel was visible. It looked like a monastery on a cliff, unusually dark even in the moonlight, and barren of activity. He saw the stairs beyond the gate but could not trace where they led. He saw the outline of a landing, and above it a row of shuttered windows. What seemed a two-story building here would be almost four stories tall elsewhere. Like many other structures in town, the lodge had to be constructed on a steep incline, buttressed on angled stilts, carved into the rocks where possible, hanging perilously over the edge at places. Elongated height deformed its features, but the kinks, bulges and blemishes were draped cleverly with vine just as a beard might mask a pockmarked face. Moonlight over the structure cast bizarrely oblique shadows, in and out of which the creepers glided when swayed by breeze. A sweet scent lingered about. Except for the steady rhythm of the sea, all was strangely quiet.

A click. A light was switched on above the landing. Moments later, Paolo heard footsteps descending the stairs. He stiffened.

It was Gabi. She came out with a lanky man, perhaps in his mid-fifties, who saw Paolo and offered a wide, warm smile across his salt-and-pepper goatee. "Ah, I have been expecting you," said the man. "I waited for some time and then I thought I should go to bed because maybe you are not coming tonight. I thought maybe you changed your mind or you were stuck somewhere, so so I went to bed. I'm glad you arrived finally. Welcome to Villa Nettuno."

Paolo shook his extended hand and offered pleasantries of his own. The innkeeper helped them unload the luggage, and asked them to park the car in a garage a few blocks up the street. On their way there, Paolo asked Gabi if all had gone well during her initial foray into the place, and she replied affirmatively—and with excitement.

"Still, I shouldn't have left you there," Paolo remarked. "I should've come with you."

"It was a little dark and scary at first, going up the stairs," said Gabi. "But, you'll see, it's lovely." She paused. "You know what's strange? That man said he had gone to bed but he answered the door almost as soon as I rang the bell, as if he was standing there. And he looked well-kept; he wasn't dressed in nightwear."

"Hmm, that is strange," said Paolo.

They walked back from the garage, and found that their host had already taken their bags inside the premises. Gabi invited Paolo in, and opened the gate for him. "It's such a lovely setting here," she said.

Paolo followed her. The stairs turned right almost immediately beyond the gate, and a long row of steps headed up, hugging the building's outer walls. A canopy of vine covered the staircase and infused the path with an alluring sweet aroma.

"Remember the scent in that overlook where we stopped?" Gabi asked.

Paolo nodded. The vines bore lush purple flowers in thick bunches, left to grow in abandon. "Smell them," Gabi whispered, pulling a branch in rich bloom. "Aren't they wonderful? I thought at first that they were lilacs."

"They're not lilacs?"

"No, wisteria. They're wisteria. They are everywhere here." Gabi was beaming. Paolo felt happy. He took a deep breath and hurried up the steps to catch up to Gabi, who had already reached the landing. "Look," she pointed outside. The vine had thinned and parted like curtains—and through it the pulsating sea was in full view, magnificent and untainted. Nothing stood between their delightful perch and an endless expanse of waves glistening in the moonlight. They stood enthralled, side-by-side, in serenity.

"Imagine waking up to the sea every morning and breathing in the scent of wisteria," said Gabi after some time.

Paolo sighed. "I wish we could stay more than two days."

"We'll have to come back."

They climbed another long flight of stairs to find themselves on a whitewashed hallway. A lantern dangled from the high cathedral ceiling. A door was ajar to their right.

"Hello?" Gabi called out.

"I'll be with you in a second." The innkeeper's friendly voice came from somewhere inside.

Paolo stepped up to the door and peered in. It looked like the cluttered living space of a small apartment; nothing like a hotel lobby. "Someone else is there," he whispered. Gabi walked up to him to see. There was a kitchen in the back, where an old woman was hunched over an ancient stove, attending a kettle.

Gabi pushed up against Paolo—and slipped. The woman heard the rustle and turned, revealing a scowling face weathered with countless wrinkles. But her eyes were startlingly alert, intense gray eyes that focused on them quickly with a leaping, piercing gaze.

Both Paolo and Gabi stepped back, unsettled.

"There you are," said the innkeeper. He had appeared in the hallway, behind them, through some other entrance. "Sorry, I was upstairs. I have already taken your bags to the room. Would you like to go there now?"Paolo glanced at Gabi and nodded. They began to follow the man down the dimly lit hallway. "I have to tell you something," the innkeeper said. "The hotel is very full this weekend, so we don't have the standard room that you requested in your reservation. So I'm giving you a family suite, no extra charge. Tomorrow you will kindly move to a standard room."

"That's fine," said Gabi.

She and Paolo followed their host up a flight of stairs and arrived at a junction: one hallway turned left, lit by the same ancient lanterns that they had seen elsewhere in the hotel; the other, beyond an arched doorway, turned right, with steps leading up toward complete darkness. "This way, please," muttered their host as he took the turning to the left. "This is a very old building. It was a convent for hundreds of years. Some parts of the old building can't be used anymore, like that dark passage over there. So when you are coming down the stairs, just make sure that you are in the lighted parts, and you'll be fine." Paolo and Gabi looked at each other without saying anything.

After another tall flight of starts, they landed on a balcony that ran the length of the building, offering an unobstructed view of the sea. A series of pillars, old and cracked, rose from the gray cement floor to support the ceiling as well as a tangled network of vines with wisteria in full bloom.

Several rooms lined the balcony, but all the doors and windows were shut.

"This is the second floor," said the innkeeper.

"Wow, just the second floor?" remarked Paolo. He walked over to the balcony and looked down. "We are already so high up."

The innkeeper laughed. "Many people have that reaction, my friend. We live on a mountain. We have to adjust to it. It doesn't adjust to us. This was the top floor of the original building. All the rooms are taken here. We added one more floor two years ago. That's where your room is. It's new and modern. You'll like it."

They followed the innkeeper to the third floor, walked through a white-washed corridor, and arrived, at the very end of the hotel, to their suite: two large rooms with large wooden windows. The furnishing was sparse: two single beds and a nightstand in the first room and only a desk in the second. The innkeeper proudly showed them the white-tiled bathroom, with a tub and "all modern amenities." He opened the windows. The refreshing seaside atmosphere instantly flooded their space. "A great view, isn't it?" remarked the innkeeper with pride in his voice.

"Do we have a balcony?" inquired Paolo. Gabi walked off to explore the other room.

"No, only the second floor has a balcony. But that's a common balcony. Everybody on that floor uses it."

"I see," said Paolo. Well, thank you. The room is great."

The innkeeper nodded, bid good night, and walked out gracefully.

Paolo sat down on one of the beds. "So here we are," he said.

"It's beautiful," said Gabi.

"Looks like we're sleeping separately on these dormitory beds. I wish they had just one bigger one."

"Small, separate beds are standard all over Europe," said Gabi with a smile. "The man said we have to move out of the room tomorrow. Do you want to try the second floor, with the balcony?"

"Yes, let's look at that tomorrow." Paolo stretched and yawned. "I'm tired, from all that driving."

"I'm a little woozy from the driving, too. Let's go to sleep, and get an early start. I'll set the alarm."

"Don't set the alarm," said Paolo. "We're on vacation. I want to get up whenever I wake up naturally."

"I want to get the most out of the day," said Gabi. "There's a lot to see. We can't just sleep in."

"But I don't want to have to wake up at a certain time and follow a routine. Otherwise what's the difference between work and holiday?"

"The difference, Paolo, is where we are. We are waking up not to go to work but to enjoy this place."

"Okay, whatever." Paolo got up andwalked into the bathroom.

"Don't say 'whatever'," exclaimed Gabi, shaking her head. She opened the guidebook and tried to read, managing only a mechanical motion to occupy her fingers and eyes on a hodgepodge of images and words that failed to engage her mind.

Paolo came out after a few minutes. "The bathroom's all yours," he said, walking up to the window. "Do you want the windows open or closed for the night?"

"I don't care," said Gabi.

Irritated, Paolo looked at her, then proceeded to close one of the windows. "I know you usually like them closed, but there's a nice breeze out there. So I'm going to leave one of them open."

"Fine." Gabi put the book down, went over to her suitcase, and began to take out the clothes she would wear the next day.

Paolo lay down on the bed farthest from the window. "Which bed do you want?" he asked.

"Either one will do," said Gabi.

"Good night," said Paolo. He sighed and turned to face the wall.

II

As it turned out, an alarm, that relic from everyday urban working life, was unnecessary. The inlet offered by the sole open window was enough: Paolo and Gabi's hard-earned retreat exploded with sunlight, a boisterous chirrup of birds, and forceful gusts of air as soon as morning broke. They woke up, surprised by the vigor around, and content, having slept soundly, if separately. Gabi flung open all the other windows, and Paolo, leaning sideways on his bed, watched a breathtaking spectacle of towering mountains lapped by the sea unfold before them, pane by pane, until they were enclosed by the endless view.

"My God!" exclaimed Paolo as he got up. "Is this how days begin here!"

"It's amazing," said Gabi under her breath.

In silent teamwork, they began to get ready, washing their faces, putting on clothes for the day, packing away miscellaneous items, all as quickly as possible, as though commanded by an unseen force. Paolo took out his camera, another object bought right before the trip, and Gabi found the batteries. Gabi pulled out their new socks from the suitcase while Paolo laid out the new walking shoes. They were driven. The disjuncture of their modernity and the insignificance of their existence against their magnificent, inexorable backdrop seemed to have provided, strangely enough, a sense of unity, even a surge of energy. They wanted to rush out, surrender themselves, and greet their fate. They had never felt an urge quite like this.

All packed up for the day, they came down the stairwell and walked to the balcony on the second floor. The view was irresistible; the mountains seemed closer, the sea louder. They sat on old wrought iron chairs, looked around in awe, walked over to different spots, breathed in the scent of the wisteria, and took pictures, alternating the setting between the mountains and the sea. Then they rearranged the chairs and sat down again, restlessly, visibly satiated yet craving more.

"We have to stay on this floor tonight," said Gabi after some time.

"Yes, absolutely," replied Paolo.

"Let's tell the innkeeper now," Gabi proposed, and they got up. Coming farther down the stairwell, they paused at the landing where another staircase, beyond an arched threshold, joined the main one. It was still dark and uninviting, surprisingly impervious to the bright daylight that splashed elsewhere. Paolo walked through the arch and looked up, unable to see where it ended. He was about to climb a few steps when Gabi tugged at his shirt: "Don't go there. Francesco told us not to."

Paolo frowned and looked at Gabi. "Who's Francesco?"

"The man who owns this hotel," said Gabi.

"Oh, he never told me his name."

"He didn't tell me either. But I saw the name stitched on a shirt that was hanging in the reception when I first came in here last night."

Paolo stepped down. "Let's find him," he said.

They walked into the reception area in the first floor and rang the bell on the counter. No one came out. "Francesco?" Paolo called out. No one answered.

"Maybe he's in that apartment, you know, where we saw that old lady?" suggested Gabi. They walked across the hallway to the apartment and found its door shut. They knocked and waited a minute. No one answered.

"That's strange," said Paolo.

"I think they are all busy with their chores," Gabi said. "Let's go outside now. We'll find him later."

They walked out of the hotel into a bustling street. Paolo asked Gabi to stand in front of the gate, under the Villa Nettuno sign, and took a picture. He panned up and zoomed in to take shots of different sections of the hotel, which were now clearly visible, jutting out of the rocks, adorned in the light purple of the wisteria. He found the second floor balcony, and way up, some windows of the third floor, but could not tell which ones were theirs. He took a few more pictures and hurried up to Gabi, who had walked off along the street in the meantime. "You know what's strange," said Paolo. "Francesco told us the hotel was full, which is why we were given a third floor suite. But all this time, we didn't see a single person anywhere in the hotel."

"Yes, I was thinking the same thing," Gabi remarked.

"I want to show you something." Paolo took the digital camera and clicked through till he found pictures of the balcony. "Look at the windows on the rooms on that balcony," he prompted.

"The shutters are all closed!" observed Gabi.

"Yes, we didn't notice it when we were there because we were focused on the view outside."

"Why would all the windows be shut on such a beautiful day?"

"Exactly."

Gabi thought for a second. "You know, it's probably nothing. Everyone must have got up and left much earlier than we did. They wouldn't leave the windows open with their valuables in the room."

"The windows have grilles," said Paolo. "Plus, we opened all our windows to take in the view. That's the first thing we did. Why wouldn't others do the same? Plus, we got up pretty early, too."

"I don't know. I don't think it's anything to be worried about."

"I'm not worried. I just think it's strange; that's all."

"It is. But come now, I want to go down that path toward the water," said Gabi, pointing to a narrow staircase that descended steeply from the street level to the waterline through rows of buildings set snugly next to one another.

Compiler's Note: The rest of the story is left to the reader's imagination, as the author was unable to finish it.

cambridge resolution

After Jalal Alamgir's sudden departure in 2011
the City of Cambridge adopted a formal resolution
in response to the outpouring of grief from
the community around him

CCM-101

City of Cambridge

R-2.

IN CITY COUNCIL
December 12, 2011

COUNCILLOR SIMMONS
COUNCILLOR CHEUNG
VICE MAYOR DAVIS
COUNCILLOR DECKER
COUNCILLOR KELLEY
MAYOR MAHER
COUNCILLOR REEVES
COUNCILLOR SEIDEL
COUNCILLOR TOOMEY

WHEREAS: Dr. Jalal Alamgir, an Associate Professor of Political Sciences at the University of Massachusetts, Boston, a political activist and Cambridge resident has died; and

WHEREAS: A brilliant and soft spoken professor with a self-effacing dispensation, an unparalleled dedication to his students and colleagues, and a strong commitment to social justice, Dr. Alamgir's death is a shock to the university community; and

WHEREAS: Dr. Alamgir stayed in touch with many of his students long after they completed their studies at the university; and

WHEREAS: Dr. Alamgir's courses on globalization and international development, world politics and world order, international relations and the politics of south Asia, were very popular in the Department of Political Sciences; and

WHEREAS: The scion of a prominent political family that endured years of persecution in his native Bangladesh, Dr. Alamgir's varied academic interests included: democratization, the interaction between economic globalization and representational politics, international relations, South Asian politics, and constructivism; and

WHEREAS: Dr. Alamgir received tenure last year and was poised to become the next director of the International Relations Program in the Department of Political Sciences; and

WHEREAS: Dr. Alamgir was founder and Principal of Red Bridge Strategy, a consulting firm on global strategy, global sales and marketing, and international legal services; and

WHEREAS: Prior to joining the faculty of UMass, Boston, Dr. Alamgir held research appointments at the Watson Institute for International Studies at Brown University, the Southern Asian Institute at Columbia University, and the Center for Policy Research, New Delhi; and

WHEREAS: Dr. Alamgir's book titled India's Open-Economy Policy: Globalism, Rivalry, Continuity was well received and was designated by the Think Tank, Asia Policy, as recommend reading for its 2008 Policy Maker's Library; and

WHEREAS: A prolific essayist, Dr. Alamgir's work was featured in many journals including: International Studies Review, Asian Survey, Asian Studies Review, Brown Economic Review, the Journal of Contemporary Asia, the Journal of Bangladesh Studies and the Journal of Social Studies. Dr. Alamgir's work was also published in magazines such as Foreign Policy, Current History, the Nation, China Daily, Global Post and the Daily Star; and

WHEREAS: Dr. Alamgir received his Doctorate from Brown University in 2000 and completed his undergraduate Studies at Saint Lawrence University, where he majored in Economics and Government; and

WHEREAS: Judging from the outpouring of grief from students and faculty in the University of Massachusetts, Boston, it is apparent that Dr. Alamgir had a profound impact on the university community and will be missed. It is also apparent that Dr.Alamgir's ideas will continue to flourish through his students who are a testament to his enduring legacy; and

WHEREAS: Dr. Alamgir is survived by his wife Fazeela Morshed, his parents M.K Alamgir and Mrs. Sitara Alamgir in Bangladesh, his colleagues at the University of Massachusetts, and hundreds of former students; now therefore be it

RESOLVED: That the City Council go on record extending its condolences to the Alamgir family, the University of Massachusetts community, and the Bangladeshi community in Cambridge on the death of Dr. Jalal Alamgir; and be it further

RESOLVED: That the City Clerk be and hereby is requested to forward a suitably engrossed copy of this resolution to Fazeela Morshed, M.K Alamgir and Mrs. Alamgir, and to the University of Massachusetts, Boston, Department of Political Sciences on behalf of the entire Council.

In City Council December 12, 2011.
Adopted by the affirmative vote of seven members.
Attest:- D. Margaret Drury, City Clerk.

A true copy;

ATTEST:- D. Margaret Drury

D. Margaret Drury
City Clerk

www.ingramcontent.com/pod-product-compliance
Lightning Source LLC
LaVergne TN
LVHW011029110826
845149LV00015B/3345

* 9 7 8 1 9 7 0 3 2 1 1 0 4 *